I0681928

MURDER IN A SMALL TOWN
THE SECRET OF CRIPPLE CREEK

∞

A novel by
Anita M. Braun
&
Timothy M. Braun

Sangre de Cristo Publishing, Inc.
Cripple Creek, Colorado

This book is a work of fiction. The names, characters, and incidents are the product of the author's imagination. Any resemblance to actual events, or persons is entirely coincidental. Many of the locations mentioned in the book are actual places in Cripple Creek, Colorado.

No part of this book may be reproduced, transmitted in any way, stored in a retrieval system, or otherwise without prior permission of the copyright holders except as provided by USA copyright laws.

Printed in the United States of America

Cover design by
Timothy M. Braun

Published by
Sangre de Cristo Publishing, Inc.,
P.O. Box 1003, Cripple Creek, CO. 80813

Dedication

Timothy and Anita dedicate this book to our respective parents and our large families. Without their love and dedication throughout the years we would not be who we are.

A Special Thanks

Thanks to Sarah Bowe Jansson, for the cover photo taken at the historic *Old Homestead House* in Cripple Creek, CO. and for her permission to use it.

Acknowledgements

Thanks to all the members of "Writing Above the Clouds" writer's critique group, especially Sandi Sumner, author of *Women Pilots of Alaska*; Leah Persons, Kari Wainwright, Natalia Brothers, Author of Soul of the Unborn, and Kathryn Veres, who gave us immeasurable guidance and support.

Thanks to Belinda, "B", for finding Sarah after 21 years!

PROLOGUE

I arrived in Cripple Creek in 1993 after being forced to retire from the Worcester, Massachusetts fire department. I was depressed after being involved in an accident during a 5-alarm fire and was looking for a small town to settle down in.

I happened upon the quaint little city of Cripple Creek while exploring Colorado and the western states. The vistas were incomparable; a green valley surrounded by snowcapped mountains above the tree line to the north and south of the city. The cleanest air you could ever find and where you can see forever, I couldn't even have imagined the secrets the small city held or would yield.

How could this have happened in my town? In a small picturesque mountain resort of just over twelve hundred residents, you'd like to think you know each and every person, and every little thing that is going on.

I knew all the gossip; who was doing whom, who was getting divorced, who was pregnant, who was contemplating running for office, who was about to get canned, etc., etc., etc.

Was I deceived, or was I just plain naïve? As the editor of the local newspaper for the past ten years, is there anything that I should have known; clues I totally missed that would have changed the course of events? Could I have really changed what happened?

How did such a closely guarded secret organization unravel so quickly, and with so much violence? How did they manage to keep such a secret, and for so long?

How could I have been so blind, so taken in by people I knew, trusted, and respected? I had the power, the influence, the fortitude, and the means.... Maybe I just didn't have the facts.

You see, newspaper editors must have the facts, the cold hard facts. They must not, and cannot be influenced by advertisers, by politics, by status, by personal relationships, by society, by... complacency.

I was.

CHAPTER ONE

Norma was busy pulling the deposit bags out of the night drop box when she heard a knocking at the bank's front door. She looked at her watch.

"We're not open yet," she yelled across the bank.

The knocking and muffled yelling continued.

Norma walked over to the front double doors. A neatly dressed middle-aged man with a white jacket, black jeans and a baseball cap stood outside, frantically motioning as if he needed a phone. Norma unlocked the inside double doors and went into the foyer.

"It's Saturday, you'll have to go over to the drive-through and we won't open for another hour. Come back then," she yelled through the outer doors.

"There's a bad accident down the block. Call the police!" the gentleman yelled back. "And call for an ambulance! They're bleeding badly!"

Norma unlocked the outer door. "Where? Where is it?" she asked looking down the street.

Before she could ask anything else, the man pushed her back into the bank foyer. He locked the outside door and grabbed her by the arm.

"Ouch, let me go!" Norma yelled trying to pull away.

"Calm down, give me what I want and I won't hurt you."

"You can't be in here, it's against the law."

"I know that. Don't worry; I'll be gone in a couple minutes. What kind of recording devices does the bank use?"

"Why?"

"Don't worry about why, just answer the question."

"And if I don't?"

The man pulled a small revolver from under his jacket behind his back and placed it against her head.

"I told you to give me what I want and no one would get hurt. If you don't, someone *will* get hurt."

Norma nodded her head. "It's, it's a digital CD recorder." She stuttered.

"Where is it?"

"Over there, in Sandra's office, in the cabinet."

"Take me."

Norma led the man into the bank manager's office and opened the cabinet. The man viewed the CD recorder for a moment and then pushed the stop and eject button. The CD ejected and the man placed it in his pocket.

"Can I sit down," Norma asked, "I'm not feeling good."

"Over there," he said pointing to the chair behind a desk. "Now, where are the CD's from the past few days?"

"In the drawer below."

The man opened the drawer, looked at the dates on the CD cases and stuffed several of them in his pocket.

Norma reached under the desk and pushed a small button.

For many years Cripple Creek's high valley, at an elevation of 9,494 feet, was considered no more important than a cattle pasture. Many prospectors avoided the area after the Mount Pisgah hoax, a mini gold rush caused by salting (adding gold to worthless rock).

On the 20th of October 1890, Robert Miller "Bob" Womack discovered rich ore and the last great Colorado gold rush began. Thousands of prospectors flocked to the region, and before long Winfield Scott Stratton located the famous Independence lode, one of the largest gold strikes in history. In three years, the population increased from five hundred to ten thousand by 1893. Although $500 million worth of gold ore was mined from Cripple Creek, Womack died penniless on 10 August 1909.

CHAPTER TWO

"Headquarters to Sergeant Majors."

"Go ahead."

"You've got an alarm at the bank."

"Again? I thought they fixed that."

"They supposedly did."

"10-4, on it."

"Bank alarm?" asked Officer Chris Sanborn.

"Yeah. It's been a while since that damn alarm's gone off. They're always false, so no big hurry. There was a string of them months back, and the bank finally had the alarm system repaired. There hasn't been any since, false or otherwise. They really need to get that fixed once and for all."

They took their last swallows of coffee, paid for their breakfast at the Two Mile High Casino on Bennett Avenue, and headed out to their cruisers.

"You take the back, I'll take the front," Majors radioed Chris as he mentally reviewed the departmental procedure for the bank alarm while heading to the bank. From the time they received the call to the time of arrival at the bank, was approximately seven minutes.

Sergeant Frank Majors was the senior officer on the department; he had been there a little over five years. Officer Sanborn was the new-guy on the job only being there for a few months.

Following departmental procedure, the two officers positioned their cruisers outside the bank at the east and west corners, front and rear of the bank. There were two entrances to the bank and these positions effectively blocked any exit from anyone who may be in the bank and gave the officers a total view.

"Headquarters to Sgt Majors."

"Go ahead."

"I've called the bank several times. There's been no answer."

"Give it another try."

As the officers waited for final word from the station, a brown Ford Escort pulled into the rear parking lot. Out jumped a slight young woman, seemingly in a big hurry, fumbling with her keys, purse and jacket while striding purposefully toward the bank's back door.

Sanborn jumped out of his cruiser. "Hold up there," he yelled pointing to the young woman.

"Why, what's going on? I work here and I'm late," she stated anxiously.

"You say you work here? What's your name?"

"My name's Lacy Whitmore and I'm *so* late for work," slowing her pace as she approached Sanborn, "I hope Ms. O'Brien doesn't fire me."

"Lacy, the bank's alarm is going off and we're checking it out right now. Please get back in your car until I tell you it's okay to go in. It's probably a false alarm."

Lacy shrugged her shoulders, turned around and slowly went back to her car looking quizzically back at the bank.

"Sarge, there's still no answer at the bank," came the voice over the radio.

"10-4."

"Chris, I'm going to check the front door," Majors radioed his partner.

With his weapon drawn, Majors inched towards the front wood-framed glass doors and tried the door latch, while Officer Sanborn went to the rear door.

"Chris," Majors whispered into his mic, "the front door is unlocked!"

After making careful observation of the interior of the bank through the glass doors, Majors radioed Sanborn, "I don't see anyone moving around inside, I'm going in."

"The back door is still locked," Chris replied. "I can't back you up!"

His senses on high alert, he stepped inside the front foyer. He quickly scanned the area, and, observing nothing out of the ordinary, crossed the floor of the bank to the rear door and unlocked it. He let Officer Sanborn in, relocking the door behind him. The two officers knew the front door should have been locked, as the bank wasn't open yet, which made them even more cautious and on edge. Both did a careful check of the building, watching for any signs of movement. There was none.

"Norma, Norma, are you in here?" Majors yelled. He knew she was supposed to be working this morning as she always did on Saturday mornings.

That was one of the nice things about a small community, thought Majors, *they knew who was supposed to be there and when.* Besides, Norma's pink Honda Prelude was in the rear bank parking lot where it resided every Saturday morning. You couldn't miss that car, it stuck out like a red pepper in a jar of pickles, and she was often ribbed about it.

The officers could find no one, no Norma, no movement, and no robbery in progress. "Looks like another false alarm," Sanborn stated as they each holstered their weapons.

Although the bank was relatively small, everything looked normal, nothing seemed out of place. The only thing missing was Norma.

The final rooms to be inspected were the manager's office and the vault. The office door was locked and the officers could detect no movement or sound on the other side of the door. The vault could only be opened by Norma or the bank manager.

Majors called the station. "The bank seems secure except for the vault and manager's office; the door's locked. Norma's not here. Call the bank manager, find out who was supposed to be working this morning and tell her we need to get into her office."

Majors turned to Officer Sanborn, "Norma's always here on Saturday mornings and her vehicle is in the parking lot. Something's not right."

"Think she walked over to a casino for a coffee and forgot to lock the door?" asked Chris.

"Could be, but I doubt it. She's too careful."

Sanborn knew the bank could not really be considered "secure" until every room had been searched and the bank vault checked.

***

It took about twenty minutes for the bank manager, Sandra O'Brien, to arrive. She yawned as she entered through the front doors of the bank; went over to the alarm on the wall behind the teller's area and entered her code, which reset it.

"Hey, Sandra! Did we get you out of bed?" Majors ask her with a devilish smile.

Her disheveled appearance suggested she had still been asleep when the station called her. She wore no make-up and her clothes looked as though she had slept in them. She answered him with a one-fingered salute.

Sandra was a textbook type-A personality; a no-bullshit, all business, meticulous woman who didn't have time for laziness or stupidity. When she asked for something to be done, she expected it to be executed without question or delay

"The alarm indicates it was set off from inside my office," Sandra stated to Majors, as she tossed the keys to him so he could open the office, "it's the large brass key. Something probably fell off a shelf or some paprs blew around and set off the alarm. The air blowing from the furnace has done it before. I'm going to make a pot of coffee."

"That alarm hasn't gone off for almost two months," she declared to Majors. "I'll call the alarm company and have it checked again if it's not the hot air blowing around. I really don't like coming down here on my day off. By the way, aren't Norma and Lacy here yet?" she asked looking around the bank.

"Lacy's out in the parking lot. She got here about twenty minutes ago. I told to stay in her car," offered Sanborn. "As for Norma, her car is here, but we haven't seen her."

As Sandra filled the coffee pot with fresh water, Majors placed the key in the office door lock and twisted the knob.

"Oh, shit!" Majors yelled from the office.

"Headquarters, get me an ambulance over here now!" Majors shouted into his radio as he keyed his mic. "Call the chief and tell him to get down here right away."

Directing his attention to his partner, and pointing to the manager, he yelled, "Chris, get her out of here now and secure the doors."

"What's going on?" Sandra asked. "I'm the bank manager, you can't just throw me out!"

Officer Sanborn escorted Sandra to the front door, "Look, I don't know what's going on yet, but it can't be good. You have to leave. Give me your cell phone number in case we need to reach you later."

Sandra dug out a business card and handed it to him. "Make sure you call me and give me a heads up. I have to report to my bosses, too. I don't want them finding out anything before I tell them"

"I will," he replied. He then locked the front door, securing the bank.

****

Sandra walked around to the rear of the bank to speak to Lacy.

"What's going on?" Lacy asked, "How come they won't let me in?"

"They just forced me out," stated Sandra, "I don't know what they found, but they kind of went off the wall when they opened my office door and called for an ambulance. There must be something wrong with Norma. I hope she's all right." She paused looking at the bank. She tapped on Lacy's car, "You might as well go on home until I call you."

"Okay, give me a call on my cell. I'm going to get some breakfast first." Lacy started her car and left.

Sandra returned to her vehicle, started it, and sat with the engine running for a few minutes staring at the bank, and then slowly drove away.

***

Although the ambulance had been called and was on its way, Majors knew no amount of medical treatment would be of any help. The person in the office was already deceased. A quick inspection showed the female had been shot in the right temple twice; blood and brain matter were splattered all over the walls, the floor, the white ceiling, and the desk. He knew that legally he was not qualified to make a pronouncement of death; only the paramedics or medical examiner could do that. And, it *was* Norma.

Sanborn, having escorted Sandra out, came into the office. He recoiled at the sight that greeted him.

"How could anyone do this to Norma?" he asked aloud. "This can't be happening in Cripple Creek!" He felt bile rising in his throat and rushed to the restroom. This was his first murder scene, and it was gruesome. Breakfast didn't taste as good the second time around.

It had been over ten years since the last murder in Cripple Creek. The only major crimes in the city since then had been a couple of sloppy attempts at robbing the more popular casinos, a few suicides, and a reported rape here and there, but no homicides.

***

Chief Reginald Campbell got to the bank about fifteen minutes after Major's request for him went in to the station. Upon arrival, he observed the two police cruisers parked at the opposite corners of the bank, and an ambulance in the front of the bank with its emergency lights flashing. He was wondering what the commotion was about, why the ambulance was there, and why they had called him. He thought maybe someone had had a heart attack or a stroke and he was ready to chew some ass for calling him in on a Saturday morning.

Sergeant Majors unlocked the front door and let the chief in. He escorted him over near the office entrance where the two paramedics were packing up their gear.

Majors never got a chance to brief him.

"Why'd you call me down here?" yelled the chief, irritation coloring his jowls.

"Call the M.E., there's nothing we can do," stated Jake, the senior paramedic, to Majors and the chief as he headed for the front door. "God damn it! Who could do such a thing to Norma?"

"Norma? What the hell's going on?" the chief blurted out, now somewhat confused.

The chief pushed his way through the paramedics and went into the office. He stood transfixed for a few seconds at the grotesque scene of blood and brain on sage green walls. "Hey you guys, wait up a minute," he yelled to the paramedics.

They both turned to face the chief. "Both of you, keep your mouths shut about this. An information blackout is in effect for this crime scene as of now. Neither of you are to breathe a word about it to anyone. It could affect the investigation if details get out," he reminded them. "Write your reports and forward me a copy. Show them to no one. You **_do not_** talk to the press. I'll talk to your boss. Got it?"

The paramedics nodded their understanding and left. Everyone knew better than to disobey a direct order from the chief, even if he wasn't in their chain of command. They also knew he would bring the wrath of God down upon them if they disobeyed his orders.

***

Chief Campbell was a short, roly-poly, cigar-smoking good-ole boy. His baldhead matched the roundness of his generous stomach protruding out from under his chest. He loved his thirty-dollar Cuban cigars and everyone had always wondered where and how he obtained them. He never told a soul.

Many in the past underestimated the chief, and he liked it that way. His mind was sharp, but it wasn't obvious by his attire or mannerisms. He was a very "law and order" type of guy; that is, order was maintained in the city by 'Reggie's' law.

He made it his daily mission to know everything that was going on in the city and nothing seemed to get past him. His list of informants was extensive and read like a criminal court docket on a busy day, with many of those informants ratting each other out in a cross network. This ensured that Reggie always knew who was doing what, and who was doing whom. He took particular pleasure from the latter and kept extensive records--he never knew when they might come in handy.

Many who partook of the local underground activities in town avoided arrest and possible jail time by staying on the right side of the chief. He alone determined who went before the local district court and faced fines or jail; who went before the local magistrate where things could be "taken care of"; and those who worked for him, and didn't go in front of any judge.

***

Majors could see the chief was really pissed off. His face was red and his voice tense.

"Damn-it, damn-it, damn-it!" the chief yelled.

Sanders had never seen the chief this irate.

"Mike, why is the chief so pissed off? I can understand he may have been friends with Norma, but it seems more than that," he whispered to Majors.

Majors whispered back, "Well, besides ruining a long running record of no homicides, he's going to have to call in the County Sheriff's Investigators, the Colorado Bureau of Investigation, and the department he despises most of all, because the murder was in a bank, *the FBI*. This isn't going to sit well with him by a long shot. They're going to steal his thunder, his absolute authority in the city. Besides, this is the day he always goes fishing."

***

The chief hated the FBI. Years earlier they had come to his city to investigate multiple complaints of corruption and civil rights abuse in his police department. They tried to act like his best buddy, 'compatriots in crime fighting, you know,' in their coy attempts to obtain any information they could about the complaints.

After several weeks of arm-twisting and interviews, the F.B.I. left empty-handed. No sane resident would breach the code of "Reggie's law."

The chief knew they were after him, and he played them as well as they tried to play him. His grip on the city tightened and was even more pronounced by the time the FBI left. Many thought he was untouchable, himself included.

In 1896 Cripple Creek suffered two disastrous fires. The first occurred on April 25 destroying half of the city including much of the business district. Four days later another fire destroyed much of the remaining half. The city was rebuilt in a period of a few months; most historic buildings today date back to 1896. After the fires, many downtown buildings were built with brick. Today, many of those buildings had to be torn down as the brick was soft and the bases of the buildings were deteriorating and deemed structurally unsafe.

By 1900, Cripple Creek and its sister city, Victor, were substantial mining communities.

CHAPTER 3

"Mama, Papa, I've been accepted to study in the United States!" Tao announced to her parents as soon as she opened the official notice containing her student visa. She was going to Colorado to study English. Her dream of becoming a translator was just an ocean away. She couldn't wait.

"Oh Tao, we're so happy for you," her mother said as she gave her a hug.

Her father grunted his agreement. America offered opportunities to a young Chinese woman that China never could.

***

Tears of joy streamed down Tao's cheeks as the plane touched down at Denver International Airport. She literally pinched herself to ensure it was real.

She collected her bags at the carousel, went through customs, and then went to find the shuttle that would take her to Colorado Springs. To her surprise there was a young man holding a sign with her name on it. She smiled. Her parents must have arranged this for her.

"Hi, I'm Tao Yang." She greeted the young man.

"Come with me. Your car is waiting." He said as he placed her bags on a cart and pulled them along.

Tao followed him to a black limousine. He opened the back door for her as she got in.

"Hello Tao." Came a voice from the darkened interior.

Tao jumped. She hadn't expected to have company.

"Who are you?" She asked.

"Not worry Tao. I here to help you settle in America life."

Tao recognized the broken English of her countryman.

"My name is Li Qiang. I work for Chinese Consulate." He was dressed in a dark suit with a deep red tie. He looked straight ahead, never at Tao.

The limo pulled away from the curb.

"How do you mean to help me?" Tao asked.

"You help China. China helps you. You help? Yes? We help you, too. We pay all your school and needs."

"What can I do? I'm here for university only. I don't think I will have time." Tao answered.

"You will make time." Li Qiang stated harshly. He leaned toward her as he took his phone out of his breast pocket. He slid the screen and showed her a picture.

"If you love them..."

Tao's hand flew to her mouth as she let out a cry. It was a picture of her mother and father in a filthy, darkened Chinese prison. The bars in the foreground, which held her parents, said everything. Her heart sank.

"What do you want of me?"

"You will be told. Not now."

Tao realized she would have no choice but to help her government in order to ensure her parent's safety. She had heard stories of a similar nature, but never believed them true. Tears of anguish replaced the tears of joy she had cried just minutes before. She was scared, for herself and for her parents.

Li Qiang leaned back and smiled a big, ugly smile. Her sobs gave him pleasure.

"You will do as you are told. It has all been arranged."

Tao swallowed. "I don't understand. Why did you choose me? Why are you holding my parents?"

"Your parents are our insurance. You do what you are told; your parents' okay. You young, beautiful, speak good English." He replied. "I show your picture at office. Everyone say you quite the China Doll.

The ride to Colorado Springs seemed to take forever. The car finally pulled up in front of an apartment building near the university's campus. Li Qiang escorted her to her new government financed home.

***

Tao sat on the sofa; face in her hands and wailed. This was not the life she envisioned. What would happen to her parents? Could she just return to China and forget it all? Would they release her parents if she did? Would they even release her parents if she did what they asked? She knew her government could not be trusted, but what options did she have?

She barely slept. The conversation with Li Qiang played over and over in her mind. Was there a way out? What if she ran away? They would not be able taunt her with her parents in prison, so they'd have no control over her. They could kill her parents and it could be a long time before she knew. Could she seek asylum? Would that save her parents?

CHAPTER 4
MONTHS LATER

June Perry rode the escalator up to the Scarlet Rose Casino's Terrace Restaurant and seated herself at their customary table. *Same old, same old,* she thought. Breakfast with the Mayor just about every morning was getting boring.

She slipped out of her black cashmere coat and draped it over her usual chair, then sat down. She pulled her cell phone out of her purse, noted the time, and checked for messages. Two minutes past eight. She was a little early.

***

Terri knew her regulars and brought a carafe of iced tea, a small canister of sugar packets and a glass, setting them down on the linen covered table in front of June.

"Good morning, June. How are you today?" went the normal morning pleasantries. She filled June's glass with the iced tea from the carafe, set it back on the table and retreated to the kitchen.

***

June had a busy day ahead of her. She glanced at her appearance in the mirrored wall behind their table. Her blond hair was pulled back in a chignon and secured with a black barrette. Her cream-colored skirt suit, trimmed in black piping, accentuated her modest curves. She wore fashionable knee high black suede boots, not very practical for temperatures in the teens, but she thought they looked good. March in the mountains could be extremely harsh. Today was one of those bitterly cold days, the kind of day to just stay home in bed.

June was tall and thin, model-like, not the stereotypical appearance one would normally associate with a librarian and town historian, her day job. She looked good and knew it, and that was a plus for her evening work.

June saw the Mayor, Daniel Comeau, approach from the back entrance. The tails of his navy blue sports coat seemed to chase him as he strode quickly across the carpeted restaurant floor. He appeared to be in a hurry this morning, moving with a purpose unlike his normal leisurely gait. June wondered if he'd missed his daily run and was trying to make up for it now. Dan had recently taken up rock climbing. He had spent most of his free time this past summer rappelling in the Garden of the Gods in Colorado Springs. He had told her he was looking forward to conquering El Capitan in Yosemite National Park next year. *Yeah, sure,* she thought. *That'll be the day!*

Terri saw Dan coming too and quickly filled his coffee cup before he reached the table, then waited to take their orders. The Mayor ordered eggs over-easy, English muffins and sausage patties. June selected pancakes topped with blueberries.

The Mayor joined June Perry for breakfast nearly everyday in an attempt to take the pulse of the community. This particular morning something was eating at him. He leaned across the table toward June, took a quick look around the restaurant, and, lowering his voice to ensure as much privacy as could be garnered at a public breakfast table, he unceremoniously broached the subject that had him so perturbed.

"I get this feeling people are talking, as though they know about 'The Club'. Do you sense that too?" His forehead was wrinkled in concern and his brown eyes searched her face in earnest as he took a gulp of sweetened coffee and waited for her response.

"Dan, I haven't heard a thing," replied June, as she stirred five packets of sugar into her iced tea, annoyed. "Are you sure you're not hearing voices? It sounds to me like you're getting paranoid again."

The Mayor's coffee cup was halfway to his mouth when he stopped abruptly and locked eyes with June.

"I am *not* paranoid," he harshly replied. Looking around again, he added, "But we really do need to keep our eyes and ears open."

June studied him but didn't say anything, though noticed that his salt and pepper hair seemed to have a lot more salt than pepper to it lately.

The waitress brought their breakfasts, set their checks on the table and quickly left to clear a table at the opposite end of the restaurant.

***

The Mayor stared at his coffee as he slowly and methodically stirred it, deep in thought. If anyone ever discovered The Red Lantern and what went on behind its walls, his career and reputation would be ruined, not to mention the likely prison time. He had to figure out a way to extricate himself from this situation. It wasn't fun anymore. There were too many people involved, and the wind could blow any which way and bring it all down around them. He wasn't sleeping well of late with this fear of discovery nagging at him. He should have stuck with respectable businesses. Normally talkative and enthusiastic, he knew he wasn't very good company at breakfast this morning.

***

June seemed lost in her own thoughts as well, and barely touched her breakfast. She mentally debated whether she should inform 'Marcos the Enforcer' again about the Mayor's latest paranoid episode. He had been 'talked to' before. The Mayor was her friend and she didn't want to cause him any trouble, but she knew 'The Club' had to be protected at all costs. She wondered if the Marcos would even allow the Mayor to get out of the business with his limbs, or even with his life intact. 'Marcos the Enforcer' wasn't interested in anyone's welfare except his own, and that of 'The Club'.

Her thoughts switched to her sons at home. She knew she had to keep up her end of the business to ensure the safety of her own family, home, and lifestyle.

June's interest in 'The Club' was both business and fun; an opportunity to act out and dress up in old-fashioned finery, which she loved. June embraced the role of Madam at The Red Lantern. The brothel members, or clientele, knew her as 'Pearl'. She had selected that moniker in honor of Pearl De Vere, the most famous Madam of The Old Homestead House during the 1890's.

Dan broke the silence, "How are the boys?"

"Thomas and Charles are doing fine. Thanks for asking."

"You know I'd really like to spend some time with Thomas. I'd like to take him fishing or hunting or something."

"We've been over this before, Dan. It's best that you don't take on a role that would confuse him. I think the relationship you two have is enough for now."

"What relationship? We don't even see each other. You keep putting me off."

"Now is not the time to discuss this. Let's work on easing your mind about the business first, then we can move on to Thomas."

They each paid their individual checks and left. Time to face the day and whatever it brought.

June went out to her car in the parking lot and sat quietly for a few minutes. She dug her phone from her purse, dialed a number and waited for a response.

"Hello, June," Marcos answered.

"Good morning. I have some information for you to consider. The Mayor may be getting paranoid again. You may want to pay him a visit."

"Thank you. I'll take care of it."

"Have a good day." June hung up. The call was succinct and to the point. No other conversation was needed.

***

After gaming was passed by a statewide vote, the residents of Cripple Creek were made up of two distinctly different groups of people, those who were from Cripple Creek ("the locals"), and those who were not.

Those who 'were not' comprised the majority of residents these days; they were here for the numerous jobs at the many casinos that made up the bulk of the local economy.

CHAPTER 5

Nightfall brought a bustling of activity *under* The Old Homestead House. The museum's curators had long gone, the lights shut off and the house secured for the evening.

But beneath the old building, keys were turned in locks, chandeliers sparkled, fire danced in the fireplace, and men and women of various descriptions entered the underground rooms of The Red Lantern. The sounds of laughter and muted conversation filled the main sitting rooms.

The Thunderhead Casino had been built right next to The Old Homestead House, a well-known parlour house of the late 1890s and now a historical museum. The casino had acquired The Old Homestead House as part of its original purchase. Downtown real estate was at a premium for buildable lots, so every available space was used.

The local Historic Preservation Society would not permit the casino's owners to move or raze the historic building, so during construction of the casino, a large basement was built under The Old Homestead House to create much needed storage space. A casino creates a tremendous amount of records that are required by the Department of Revenue to be kept for many years. An underground connective hallway was created between The Thunderhead and the space beneath The Old Homestead House accessible only by the casino's elevator. The records had to remain secure.

Unfortunately, as Cripple Creek's casino boom of the early 1990s waned and then flattened out, The Thunderhead was one of the first casualties. Mismanagement, lack of gaming experience, poor location and limited financial backing resulted in the casino's early demise and it sat empty for many years.

That is, until several locals approached the bank which now owned the building, to purchase the casino and historic brothel out of bankruptcy. Each of the principals pooled their money so that each would have a stake in the business' success or failure. To all of the investors it sounded exciting at the time, and Cripple Creek would now really re-live some of its historic past, including the flow of substantial cash into the pockets of a select few.

Due to gaming restrictions, casino owners could not hold elected office; the casino was reopened as a nightclub and hotel about two years later. It was financed, managed, and run by partners of "The Club'," as they referred to themselves.

The Thunderhead Nightclub was open for business. But it was more than a nightclub. The old storage spaces, which had been largely forgotten, were converted into a modern brothel dubbed The Red Lantern, a tongue-in-cheek reference to the red light district. There were several suites for servicing customers, a bar, a poker room and a lavishly appointed parlour room for greeting guests and lounging.

Each Club member, client and employee was issued a key card, which was swiped along a magnetic reader, to be used when riding the elevator *alone.* For everyone else, the elevator would only take them to the hotel above the nightclub or to the dance floor. Once the card data was electronically confirmed, the elevator brought the person to the underground brothel, inaccessible by any other means.

All services were paid for in full by electronic means before access to the Red Lantern was granted. Members could also be advanced large sums of cash for the poker games or for any tips or gifts they wished to bestow upon their favorite "girl".

The escorts and clients of The Red Lantern were recruited through specific guidelines drawn up by 'The Club' owners. An escort service in Colorado Springs, run by 'The Club', advertised in Colorado Spring's largest newspaper and monthly men's magazines for young women and separately for clients.

The file of any escort, after a stint with the escort service, and if meeting all of the requirements, would be secretly presented to 'The Club' as a possible recruit for the brothel. If a quorum of club partners were in agreement, the escort would be offered a brothel position, usually at double the money she currently made, plus any tips or gifts she may receive. Before an invitation was extended, however, each recruit was given a warning. If they ever revealed anything about the brothel or its location to anyone, it could result in certain death for her and possibly for her family. There could be no misunderstanding, and 'The Club' would take no chances. The money would be very good, but the punishment for breaking the rules would be very severe.

Recruitment of clients to the brothel was not much different. After someone had been a client of the escort service as a repeat customer several times, or for a specific time, and if the client had the proper level of income and passed a detailed background check, he would be considered as a customer recruit for The Red Lantern. Where such a person showed interest in such an arrangement, he would be given the same warnings as the escorts. If the potential client agreed to the terms, and the partners of 'The Club' were also in agreement, they'd be introduced to the brothel after Marcos completed another background investigation.

Anyone who knew Marcos feared him and he was recruited specifically for that reason. Only the partners knew his real name. He was a huge man, full beard and very muscular. He never smiled nor spoke unless he had to. Tattoos covered both arms and his neck and he wore only black clothing. He was intimidating to say the least and he enforced *all* the rules.

The rules were very simple:

1. Payment was expected prior to or upon entrance to the brothel.

2. What was seen or heard at the brothel stayed at the brothel.

3. Not a word was spoken outside of the brothel about the brothel or anything relating to the brothel.

4. No client may contact any of the brothel's employees outside of the brothel, or try to identify any of the employees. The escorts may not try to identify or contact any clients outside of the brothel.

5. Only 'The Club' may bring in new recruits, both escorts and clients.

In 1992, the locals of Cripple Creek who were pushing for gaming in Cripple Creek and who owned the majority of the downtown sections of the city where the casinos would be located, were fearful of the "outsiders" who came for work in the casinos. They didn't want the "out-of-towners" taking over and running 'their' city if gaming was approved.

That had to be somehow alleviated. Control of the city must be maintained. Only the locals, they believed, should control the destiny of the city and the riches gaming was sure to bring. Sure, the casinos and the owners would greatly profit, but it would be at a price; a price the city leaders would control.

CHAPTER 6

Harold "Smokey" Mann swiped his key card and rode the elevator to the basement floor.

Madam Pearl greeted him warmly, planting a welcoming kiss on his cheek as she took his coat and handed him a snifter of brandy. Pearl was decked out in a deep rose-colored gown, long black lace gloves and a cameo brooch at her throat.

Smokey complimented her, "You look stunning tonight, Pearl."

"Thank you, Sir. I hope you enjoy your evening. Let's have a seat in the parlour and Blaze will be right with us."

The flames were flickering in the fireplace, warming the parlour. The lights were low, casting a gentle glow throughout the brothel. Classical music played softly in the background and laughter emanated from the back rooms.

Smokey was a regular customer and had his favorite girl, Blaze. He didn't know her real name; customers weren't supposed to, or allowed to. It was all about fulfilling fantasy without being mired in reality.

As Smokey was enjoying his brandy and making small talk with Pearl, he saw Blaze being confronted aggressively by a man down the hallway. The man was grabbing her by the arm and trying to pull her into one of the back rooms.

Blaze was screaming, "No, leave me alone," while trying to wrench her arm from his grasp.

Smokey bolted to his feet and ran toward Blaze and her attacker. He grabbed the assailant in a chokehold until he released his grip on Blaze and gave up. The man slunk off as she went to Smokey and fell into his arms.

Blaze was a flaming redhead as her name implied, a full-bodied, flowing mane of loose curls fell to the middle of her back. Her impish face was sprinkled with delicate freckles. Her eyes were sparkling green, full of flirt and fun. She wore full-fledged Victorian circa attire, from a snugly tied corset to black lace-up ankle boots. Today her dress was a deep royal blue, trimmed in black monkey fur.

The vintage clothing enticed Smokey. He always got excited, and his heart rate increased as he thought about Blaze while he went about his daily business. Whenever he began dreaming about his next encounter, it was as though he was in a trance-induced stupor, nothing around him mattered. Smokey was a real estate mogul in the greater Denver area and he couldn't wait to make his weekly trek to Cripple Creek to be with Blaze and live out his Wild West fantasies. He would rescue the damsel in distress and then she would gratefully reward him with her body. They modified their playful rescue from time to time, but it never failed to delight and please him.

"This time," Blaze said under her breath, "everything went perfectly!"

Smokey's excitement grew as she pulled him into her room and closed the door. He unbuttoned the tiny buttons down the back of her dress. Unlacing her corset intensified his yearning, almost to the point of wanting to rip her clothes off and have her immediately, rather than taking his time and receiving his prize. His greatest pleasure in undressing Blaze was releasing her smooth milk-white breasts from her clothing's bondage. She had full curves with ample softness for a bone weary man.

Blaze was sitting on a stool with her back to him, naked from the waist up. He leaned toward her, her long curls crushed between their bodies. He kissed the nape of her neck while his hands moved to her face, gently caressing the silky smooth skin around her cheeks and lips with his fingertips. He took several deep breaths through his nostrils, inhaling the sweet smells of her hair and perfume.

"Hmmmm, Crystalle. You remembered," he softly told Blaze. He had given her the perfume years ago and she always remembered to wear it when he was expected for a visit.

Blaze had told Smokey she had a true affection for him and often looked forward to his visits. She knew how to please him and he took particular care to try and please her. He bestowed many expensive gifts upon her, as well as generous financial tips for their liaison. Theirs was an unusual relationship for the brothel, but they had developed it over a long period of time.

Smokey was so enamored with Blaze, years before he had attempted to obtain Blaze's true identity, going against 'The Club's' rules. He had almost received the information but stopped short. Warned by partners in 'The Club' that if he ever found out Blaze's true identity, he would be banned from any further contact with her, and potentially suffer painful physical consequences. This was the law of 'The Club', and he could expect that it would be upheld.

He leaned into her as he massaged her soft nipples between his fingers. She could feel his rock hard penis through his gray slacks pressed against her back. She turned on the stool and unzipped his fly. She took his cock in her hand and gently stroked it while looking into his eyes. Smokey pulled her to her feet and her dress fell from her hips to the floor. She continued to undress him as they kissed passionately while eagerly making their way to the bed.

In order for the locals to always have control of the city, at the last minute the city fathers used their influence to cause an amendment to be placed in a State statute governing gaming in Colorado. That amendment stated that no person with a gaming license may hold any elected municipal or county office in the three gaming cities or counties in which gaming was allowed, nor be allowed to be appointed to a Planning Commission.

Since just about everyone who worked in a casino had to have a gaming license, this law effectively kept anyone who came to Cripple Creek for a job in the casinos from running for or holding any elected office. It also effectively allowed several of the local families who controlled Cripple Creek to keep a tight rein on everything that went on in the city.

It allowed those families to pass ordinances that enriched themselves at the expense of the casinos, small businesses, and the residents. But, that was business.

CHAPTER 7

Pastor Brian Gray was sitting at home at his desk reconciling the church's checkbook when the phone rang.

"Hello, Pastor Gray," he said.

"Pastor, I desperately would like to speak with you privately at your earliest convenience," the caller stated.

"Desperately? Okay... I have an opening tomorrow morning at nine if that is good for you. May I have your name, please?"

"I..., I can't give it to you right now. Tomorrow you'll understand why."

"Okay, can I have your phone number in case something comes up and I may have to reschedule?"

"I'm sorry, Pastor, it may not be safe to do that either."

"Are you sure you want to talk to me? It kind of sounds like you should to talk to the police."

"I... I can't trust the police. I have something I want to reveal to you because I want to get right with God and get out of the situation. The police can't do anything for me. There are reasons. Please help me and meet with me tomorrow."

"Alright. Meet me at the church in the morning at nine."

"I know you have a lot of questions, Pastor. I hope to answer most of them tomorrow. Thank you for agreeing to meet with me."

She hung up.

Brian could sense she seemed very nervous, even scared, and this piqued his interest even more. The whole thing sounded ominous and he was anxious to find out what it was all about. Why didn't she want to relate any information over the phone and refused to leave her name or a number? He could only assume she'd show and he would get the details then.

Brian's wife Christine appeared in the office doorway.

"Is there a problem?" She asked, "I heard the phone ring."

"Not sure, but I'll need you to come to the church tomorrow morning at nine. I've just scheduled a meeting with a woman and as far as I can tell, she's no one we know."

It was the pastor's policy to never be alone with a woman other than his wife in all aspects of his personal and professional life. That policy eliminated any temptations or suggestions of impropriety and any accusations that may come with it.

He had created and imposed the policy on himself as a result of a scandal he had witnessed as a young associate pastor in Louisiana.

The senior pastor at his church had succumbed to temptations of the flesh while counseling an attractive, young divorcee, resulting in his dismissal from the church, a divorce of his own, and a congregation that was torn between forgiveness and anger. It wasn't a pretty situation and certainly could have been avoided. He had resolved that an incident of that nature would never happen to him.

***

The late March wind was merciless, and despite clear blue skies and a brilliant morning sun, there was no real warmth.

Buttoned up against the chill, Brian made short work in walking the four blocks to his church. The pastor was in great physical shape and walked to work each day. Along with walking, he worked out religiously five days per week at the local gym, lifting weights and jogging on the treadmill. He had competed on his college wrestling team and had maintained an exercise regimen since graduating ten years before.

***

Brian arrived at the church, flipped on the lights, turned up the thermostat and decided to review the sermon notes on his desk while he waited for their mystery guest to arrive.

Christine had just dropped their daughter, Madison, off at school and joined him in the office.

"What time was the appointment?" Christine asked, as she busied herself cleaning up around the office and brewed a pot of coffee.

"Nine o'clock," he responded and noted by a glance at the clock on his desk that it was quarter past. He understood about running late but wondered if she would still come or had simply changed her mind. After all, he knew 'getting right with God' wasn't always an easy thing to do.

He recognized sin was human nature and being accountable to God required facing whatever was eating away at one's mind, body and soul. He also realized that he couldn't make things right with God for her directly. That was between the sinner and Him, but he was willing to be the intermediary and help guide anyone who asked for the help.

Ten a.m. and they were still waiting. By ten-thirty they concluded she wouldn't be coming, so they turned the lights off, turned the heat down, locked up, and left for a late breakfast.

Cripple Creek, in its heydays of the 1890s, had as many as forty-five thousand residents who worked in the mines and the many small businesses, bars and brothels. The population had shrunk to about four hundred residents in 1992, when the voters of Colorado approved limited gaming for three mountain cities; Cripple Creek, Black Hawk and Central City. All three cities were historic mining towns, which, until gaming, had almost deteriorated into ghost towns. The residents of Colorado passed the Constitutional Amendment mainly for the taxes garnered from the casino to go to historic preservation.

CHAPTER 8

Tao was instructed to work at an escort service at night and attend school during the day, though her heart was no longer in her studies. Her focus was the safety of her parents. Family always came first and now anxiety was her constant companion. She was told her job was to bring documents to the Chinese Consulate in Denver whenever they were received. A client of the escort service would specifically request her, and he would hand-deliver the documents.

Tao worked for the escort service for several months turning tricks after school and transferring documents to the Consulate when she received them from one of her johns.

When Tao informed the Consulate she had been invited to work at a secretly located brothel in Cripple Creek, and she would have to give an answer soon, she was directed to take the position. The Chinese thought the transfer of documents would be easier and more secure in such a restricted place. Plus, Tao figured she would rather work there, as she wouldn't have to turn as many tricks in the brothel as she did as an escort, and that suited her just fine.

Tao was of delicate beauty. Pale, nearly pearlescent white skin; her face was framed by ebony black hair. Her dark almond eyes, wise beyond her twenty-one years, peered out from under long shaggy bangs; a characteristically flat Chinese nose and full lips graced her face. Her tiny, small-boned physique earned her the nickname "China Doll" at the brothel. She was definitely an exotic treat in a sea of Caucasians.

Her clientele were the type of men who were especially drawn to demur women, women from a culture like hers who would happily walk ten paces behind them. She reluctantly went along with the ruse, though it was a lifestyle she detested.

She had witnessed women treated very poorly in her own country and she had experienced it in many ways herself. She had hoped to get away from all of that by coming to America, but sadly it would be no different here. Once a slave, always a slave.

Tao's first meeting with her contact had been nerve wracking. She was anxious to see this through for the sake of her parents and hoped her American contact would be a compassionate man, forced to work for the Chinese under coercion like her, or face some dire hidden consequence. They would have something in common to talk about and she may not have to perform.

She had disliked him immediately. He was not friendly or personable; he was pompous and self-righteous. He obviously didn't care his worldly cravings came at her expense; he acted as though she was expendable, just one in a billion Chinese girls. She dreaded his visits. He used her just like a throw-a-way prostitute.

***

Colonel John Durham worked at NORAD. He was an eighteen-year career military man. He kept his head shaved in a 50's era crew cut style, his thick neck supporting his fat, round head atop a barrel chest.

Greed drives most people to commit crimes, whether against their loved ones or government, and it was no different for Colonel Durham. The Chinese government was paying him handsomely to assuage his financial appetite in exchange for top secret military files from NORAD.

He envisioned all of the toys he could buy with his new wealth: a new sports car, a top of the line RV, a fast boat, a new home theater, a new home for that matter. He'd prove to his father that a military career could provide a great living. Of course he knew he couldn't flaunt excessive amounts of cash without some explanation. As he was only a couple of years away from full military retirement, waiting that amount of time and then moving out of the area to someplace no one knew him would be the safest move to make. He would come up with a story about how he made his fortunes and no one would be the wiser. He had been careful in this covert mission, and was only a couple of deliveries away from the true money pot. He wasn't going to let anyone or anything screw it up for him.

This night, Colonel Durham groped Tao roughly, his Neanderthal idea of foreplay, though he really wasn't interested in having sex with the 'chink'. He was there for document drop-off only. If he hadn't had to play the brothel game, he would have walked in, handed over the documents and been on his merry way. Instead, he had to spend a reasonable amount of time in the room with China Doll to give the appearance of a happy, satisfied customer. He decided she should give him a blowjob; might as well get something out of his trip to Cripple Creek. *After all,* he thought, *her government was paying for it.*

"Come over here," he commanded Tao.

She obeyed and crossed the room to stand in front of him.

He stood up, unzipped his jeans and pulled China Doll towards him, pushing her down onto her knees as he sat on the edge of the bed. Holding her by the back of her head, he pulled her toward his crotch.

"Suck on it," he demanded.

"You must wear condom," Tao protested, "everyone must."

"Forget about the damn condoms, just suck on it."

***

China Doll tried her best to give him a quick blowjob; his cock was tiny; three and a half inches tops, even at full erection. He must have thought he heard her gag on his 'manhood,' because he came prematurely. She had actually been stifling a laugh. When she'd finished, she went to the bathroom, gargled with mouthwash and cleaned up.

"Wake me up in an hour," he commanded as he rolled over on the bed and fell asleep, snoring loudly.

China Doll took a shower and swished the mouthwash around in her mouth in an attempt to remove the taste of him. It wasn't so much the taste as the revulsion of him she wanted to remove. He was the only one of her customers she reviled and could never seem to get the stench of him off of her.

She imagined stabbing him in his fat, hairy back with a letter opener as he slept. It was something she could never do, but the anger she felt every time she saw him brought those thoughts to the forefront of her mind. She settled for the next best thing; spiking his vodka and tonic with a couple drops of Murine. She laughed to herself as she envisioned him having one hell of a bout of diarrhea on his way back to the Springs. No restrooms or port-a-potty's for miles.

Sitting on a chair across from the bed, China Doll watched the clock tick one second at a time, wishing she could speed it up so she could be rid of him.

***

Tao would have to make the trip to the Chinese Consulate in Denver tomorrow to deliver the documents. The trip was long, two hours from Cripple Creek, then two hours back; half a day spent just driving. Meeting with the Chinese agent left her feeling hopeless. He was always eager to see what she had brought and assured her that helping her country in this way would keep her family alive. They both knew that the only reward she was seeking was her parents' safe release from prison. She hadn't been in contact with them since beginning work for the Chinese government. She had repeatedly asked the consulate for proof that they were actually still alive, but had never received it. All she could do was to try and contact old friends in China for help while she continued her distasteful work, erring on the side of caution.

******

City jobs went to locals who went along with the system and kept their mouths shut. The Police Chief was appointed to head up a department that grew to over 20 officers. It didn't matter that he had no experience. He was a local and could be depended upon to "take care" of those who mattered and those the Council wanted handled with kid gloves.

The local magistrate, "the judge", who was appointed by the Council, had no law experience and had never studied law, but he was a local and could be depended upon to do the "right thing" for the "right people."

CHAPTER 9

Pastor Brian Gray and his wife Christine had been working in the garden for almost two hours since sun up, prepping the ground for planting. The rain had come early and hard, which drove them indoors. They were enjoying a breakfast of bacon, eggs and waffles when the phone rang. The golden brown waffles, smothered with butter and maple syrup, were especially tasty after working up an appetite.

"Hello. Pastor Gray," he managed to say while trying to swallow a mouthful of waffles.

"Pastor," came a subdued female voice. "I'm very sorry for missing our appointment last month."

Brian was surprised. He recognized the voice immediately as the mysterious woman who had called him weeks ago asking for his help and hadn't kept her appointment. He didn't yet know her name and it irked him that she wouldn't even be considerate enough to at least give him that.

"Who are you?" Brian inquired. "What is your name?"

"I can tell you my name when we meet," she stated, her voice barely audible. "I can't talk on the phone. Are you on a wireless phone?"

"Yes, I am," Brian answered. "Does it matter?"

There was a momentary hesitation. "May I please make another appointment, Pastor? I promise I will come this time, but I am very nervous. I have a lot to talk to you about and get off my chest," she pleaded. Again there was a momentary hesitation. "Things that are not of the ordinary."

Brian was puzzled. What did she mean, *'not of the ordinary'*? "How about noon today? Would that be a good time for you?"

"No, I can't be seen coming to your place," she replied, "and you may not want me seen at your place either after you hear what I have to say. Can we make it later, sometime after dark? I know this all sounds odd and mysterious, but believe me-it has to be this way. You'll understand after we talk."

Brian agreed to meet her at the church office at seven-thirty that night. The vague meeting topic had an ominous tone to it and he felt uneasy all day. It consumed his thoughts. He had difficulty focusing on the matters at hand while waiting to meet with the mysterious woman.

***

Brian and Christine waited for the babysitter, and then walked up to the church together. Christine headed straight for the thermostat and cranked the heat up. Brian flipped on the lights in the vestibule and office.

The church building was over 100 years old and not very well insulated. The soft pine was plentiful in Cripple Creek in the 1800s when the church was built. The interior of the church was inundated with pine: the rafters, the pews, the balcony, the floors, the doors, and bookshelves, even the pastor's desk. The desk had been worn smooth to a soft, honey sheen over the decades.

Brian often wondered, as he did now, about those who had sat at this desk before him. He knew they were not as fortunate to have a thermostat to simply adjust the church's environment or a flick of the switch on the wall to have light. In times past, they had to bring lots of wood or coal into the church for a small amount of heat and candles and lanterns for light.

Brian heard the massive wooden door swing open and felt a gust of cold air as it pushed its way into the church from the outside. He then heard a clattering of heels on the old wooden floors as the mystery woman made her way to his office. She came to his doorway and stopped, staring at the pastor's wife.

"I thought this would be confidential," she said. "This is the reason I didn't come in last month." She started to turn around.

"Please come in," Brian invited, "it *is* confidential." He stood and welcomed her in, saying, "Please, have a seat."

"Would you like some coffee or tea?" asked Christine.

"Coffee would be great," she replied and walked over to the desk, her eyes darting back and forth to Christine. She sat down on the brown padded steel chair in front of the desk, "Cream and sugar, please," she requested.

Christine had already brewed a pot of coffee. She filled two Styrofoam cups, collected some sugar, creamer and spoons and placed one before their guest and the other before Brian.

"Your red hair is beautiful," complimented Christine.

"Thank you," replied the guest, finger-combing her hair. "It's the Irish in me."

"What shall I call you?" Brian asked.

The woman hesitated, stammered and looked around warily, "Before we begin, there is one thing. What I am going to tell you, you probably won't believe and I don't feel comfortable discussing in front of your wife."

Brian explained his policy about not being alone with women other than his wife. However, he agreed in this instance that his wife would leave the room, but the door would remain unlocked and she would be in the next room.

"That will be fine," she said.

Christine smiled at her husband as she quietly let herself out of the office and closed the door behind her.

"My name is Samantha," she almost whispered after Christine had exited the room.

***

An hour later, Samantha was driving home, lighting her third cigarette. She was even more jittery, downright scared, about her situation now that she had confided in the pastor. Every noise she heard would be someone coming for her. She had to get out somehow, but how? If anyone ever knew she told about the brothel she'd be dead. Those were the rules and she had agreed with them when she decided to take employment at the brothel. Could she fake her own death? Would she be able to just take off and disappear? How far reaching was the organization? Did they have eyes and ears everywhere? She just didn't know. She could only hope that the pastor was a true man of God and would maintain his word about keeping their meeting confidential.

***

Until I started a local newspaper, in the early days of gaming and before, the city fathers made sure that only the news they wanted to get out, got out. Any news that was detrimental to the ruling families was buried and never made it out of the city. In those days, everything worked as it was supposed to.

All of the important decisions before the City Council were made well ahead of time at one of the locals' bars, where the liquor flowed freely and any problems were worked out between the competing families interests.

After I started the local newspaper, I was loved by half the residents (those here for a job) and hated by the other half ('the locals'). I reported on all the hot topics and all the decisions the City Council made. They didn't like that. At one of the local elections, most of the City Councilors were kicked out of office. The city was changing.

CHAPTER 10

The meeting with Samantha lasted about an hour. After she left, Pastor Brian walked briskly out of his office into the foyer and almost plowed into his wife.

"What's wrong, honey?" she asked, but Brian didn't seem to hear her. He appeared pale and lost in thought. She had seen that look several times before, but this time it seemed more intense.

Finally acknowledging her, and still slightly lost in his own fog, he muttered incredulously, "I, I've either just spoken with the biggest liar I have ever heard, or...." he caught himself and stopped.

"Or what?"

"I wish I could tell you even a part of what she just told me, but you know I can't. It was told to me in confidence. Just know that if it's true, there's a real, huge problem. I can't even begin to comprehend how it would affect our community."

And *that* would be the understatement of the year he thought to himself.

According to Samantha, those involved, although not named specifically, are probably some of the people he has interacted with and trusted since he moved to Cripple Creek twelve years ago. Now, whom could he really trust, he wondered?

***

Christine knew better than to press her husband for any more information. She sometimes envied the information that he received from confessions and confidential guidance sessions, but at the same time didn't want the burden it sometimes put upon him. She had seen the weight he had carried around after speaking to members of his flock in private; it sometimes kept him mentally exhausted for days and weeks as he prayed for direction. He didn't always know the answers or how to counsel some of the tougher issues.

***

The pastor paced the floor with his head down and his hand on his chin. Who could he talk to about this disclosure? Was she really telling the truth? How could he find out if it was true? How could he get the information he needed without revealing what he had heard, or the source? And, if he found it was true, what would he do? What could he do? Deep down, he hoped it was all a big fabrication, a big fat lie, but he knew he was going to have to become a part-time detective to get to the bottom of this story. Besides, why would a girl like her admit to being a prostitute and ask to be forgiven, if she really wasn't?

Brian suddenly recalled what he had learned in divinity school. If someone's life was in danger, if there was a serious threat to someone's safety, or if he felt someone was about to commit suicide, he could break confidentiality to prevent a crime or someone hurting themselves or someone else. Otherwise, he was expected to maintain the secrecy. How could he get around this without breaching their unspoken agreement and still live with himself?

***

The city of Cripple Creek had deteriorated so much during the past century; it was practically a ghost town when the residents of Colorado voted for three cities to host casino gaming. The city infrastructure had to be resurrected and rebuilt from scratch. There was only one paved road in town–State Highway 67 came through Cripple Creek from Divide, the paving ending six miles away in the small town of Victor. A new wastewater treatment plant had to be built to handle the tens of thousands of daily visitors to the city. Most of the water system in the city still used wooden water mains and due to the solid rock, they were buried so shallow that many froze up during the cruel cold of the winters, and, there were no storm drains.

CHAPTER 11

Ralf's Breakroom sits on Bennett Avenue on the east end of town. It is a combination family restaurant, bar, and entertainment center for locals packed into one location.

Ralf's is the only place in town, aside from the casinos, providing entertainment and full meals. Many visiting families go there to eat, as several of the casinos don't allow children inside. Others just like the atmosphere without the consistent noise, the ding-ding-ding the slot machines generate. Weekends usually see a small town band on Friday or Saturday nights, with karaoke on Sunday nights.

It's the home-away-from-home of Roxie Dunbar, a thirty-six year old former Cripple Creek/Victor homecoming queen, who, at eighteen years old, went off to Hollywood after high school graduation to find fame, fortune and adventure.

She returned to Cripple Creek about six years later and, when asked, she smiled and told everyone she found plenty of adventure, but no fame or fortune.

Although many years had passed since her days of popularity and glory in high school, she still retained the gleam in her eyes and the bounce in her steps. Her vitality often attracted many want-to-be, but temporary, suitors she seemed to always decline or wave off. Besides, many of them were usually pretty drunk when they got up the nerve to try to make any headway with her, which she detested.

Roxie still sported shoulder-length California bleach-blond hair, a glowing year-round tan, and several small, but noticeable tattoos gracing her back and shoulders.

It is rumored she has others, but only a chosen few have seen them. She is proud of her 38-25-36 figure and makes no bones about it.

The other full-time bartender and waiter is Ted, a tall, good-looking, 30's something burnt-out ex-baseball player who threw out his arm and was dropped before he got to the big league. Ted has a great sense of humor and loves to tease his customers. He came to Cripple Creek about nine months ago after hiking to the summit of Pikes Peak. He loves the mountains, the locals and all the hiking and biking the area offers.

***

The local School Board was not much different than the local government. Many of the local families who controlled City Hall also ran the local school district, sat on the school board, and weren't shy about placing only locals, and many relatives, in any position of authority, whether they were qualified or not. This didn't matter to most locals as long as their kids received the special attention they needed, and 'deserved', and as long as their kids dominated in all the sports programs.

CHAPTER 12

Pastor Brian picked up the phone and dialed.

"Hello," Brian recognized Chief Campbell's bark.

"Hi, Chief, this is Pastor Brian. I need to speak with you for a few minutes. Do you have time for coffee anytime this morning?" asked the pastor.

Brian had concluded that since the chief was part of his flock, maybe he could talk to him without divulging anything confidential. He figured he would try to walk the fine line without crossing it.

"Brian, how are you?" the chief's voice mellowing, "How about making it tomorrow morning, I'm really kind of tied up today."

"That sounds good. Where do you want to meet?"

"How about Ralf's, about 10 a.m.?"

"OK. Sounds good, meet you there."

Brian really didn't like going into a bar, but Ralf's was also a family restaurant, and besides, there really wasn't anywhere else to meet outside of his church or home. Most of the casinos in town had good restaurants, but he didn't like being seen in the casinos either. In the end, he had to give himself permission to go into Ralf's. That's just the way it was in Cripple Creek.

The next morning the pastor met the chief at exactly ten a.m. in Ralf's Breakroom. They seated themselves, as they were the only customers at that time of the morning. Ted was working and walked over to the table to take their orders.

"Morning, Chief. What can I get you?" asked Ted, chomping on a toothpick.

"Coffee."

"And you, Sir?" Ted asked turning to Brian.

"Coffee also, with a glass of water, please" he requested.

"I think I've seen you around town, but never in here. I'm Ted, if you need anything else, give me a yell," he said hoping to find out who was with the chief.

"Ted, meet Brian Gray. He's a pastor in town and keeps all of us on the straight and narrow," said the chief with a smile.

"Hi, Pastor, welcome to Ralf's," greeted Ted, extending his hand. Brian shook Ted's hand. "Well, let me get that coffee brewing, I'll put on a fresh pot." Ted excused himself to fill their orders.

Turning his attention to the chief, Brian began with small talk. "How have things been with you, Reggie? Everything going okay?"

"Things couldn't be better," replied Reggie. "Oh, of course there are always little things popping up, but nothing the department can't handle," he added.

"That's good to hear. Cripple Creek is such a great community, and feeling safe makes it even more comfortable," agreed Brian.

Reggie played along. "How are Christine and Madison?"

"Oh, they're great," Brian enthused. "We're all healthy and staying busy. Christine is starting a new woman's Bible study group on Tuesday nights, and Madison is taking ceramic classes. We're seeing a few new faces at the church on Sunday too."

The bartender brought their coffee then busied himself straightening tables and chairs, and putting out place settings.

Finally Brian got up the nerve to broach the subject. In a subdued voice he said, "Chief, what if I were to tell you I have information there is a high-priced prostitution ring operating in Cripple Creek, along with high-stakes illegal poker games. What would you say?"

Brian was hedging on the information. He knew he had to be careful about what he said and he wasn't a hundred percent sure he could trust anyone. Plus, Brian still wasn't sure the information he was given was completely true. He was hoping it wasn't.

"Aw, hell, Brian, this is a casino town," the chief responded, "Excuse my language, but you're always going to hear rumors of prostitution in this town. I've heard them for years, but I've never found anything credible to substantiate them."

The pastor was a little taken back by the response from the chief. In a way Brian thought he was going to shock him, or the chief would outright deny everything. Or, maybe the chief would throw a bunch of questions at him about where he heard the rumors, and he would have to fend them off, but this response took him by surprise.

Reggie continued, "We don't really have any prostitution to speak of around here. Sure, once in a while we find a druggie that wants to sell herself for a little drug money, but we usually take care of that in short order. And once in a while we'll hear about a high-price call girl working the casinos. We let the guys over at the Division of Gaming know about it and they usually take care of it. Other than that...."

"Well-," Brian started to respond.

The chief cut him off. "Does your information come from a credible source?"

Now the chief was pressing, but he thought the chief knew better than to ask for a name.

"I don't know. I haven't any idea how good or bad the information is. I really don't know the person either, so, I just thought I would ask and pass the information along. I guess I figured if there was something like that going on, you would want to know about it, and, if I kept it to myself, it would really bother me. We can't have anything like that going on in this town."

The chief looked at Brian and smiled. He knew how the pastor was, and realized it would have bothered him if he didn't report what he was told.

"I always appreciate any information that helps keep the city safe and clean, Brian."

"What about the high-stakes poker games? Heard anything about those?" Brian persisted.

"Shit..." the chief caught himself. "Sorry." He looked down at his coffee. "Every once in a while the guys over at gaming hear about an illegal poker game, investigate and bust it, but it's been awhile since they've had any of those. I think the players got the word or moved their games elsewhere," stated the chief, "but other than that, I haven't heard a thing. I don't really get too excited about poker games as the guys over at gaming enforcement usually take care of it. They just use us for backup if they think they're going to need it. I really haven't heard anything about any high-stakes games though. Most of the high stakes games I hear about are down in the Springs."

Brian noticed the chief fidgeting with his spoon and repeatedly adjusting his tie. He didn't seem nervous, but a little agitated and guarded. He also noticed the chief never looked him in the eyes when he answered. He still wasn't sure about anyone, even the chief, and didn't want to press the issue. It was time to let it go for now.

"Well, OK, I just thought I should mention it to you in case there was something to it."

The chief finished his coffee. "I really appreciate it, Brian. I have an appointment with the Mayor this morning, so I best get going. I think he wants to see me about some parking issues. Seems we've been getting a few complaints. If you hear anything further, be sure and give me a call. I'll see you Sunday."

Brian said his good-byes to the chief and stayed a few more minutes. He wanted to collect his thoughts on what had just transpired. Was the chief being honest with him? Could he trust him? Why did he seem agitated when he pushed the subject?

The pastor flashed back to the meeting with Samantha. She had told him there existed a high-priced prostitution business in Cripple Creek, and that she was one of the girls working at the brothel. The brothel was located in town, but she wouldn't say where. She said she made very good money working part time, but decided she didn't want to work there anymore. The problem was she didn't know how to end it. She had heard through the grapevine that other girls had suddenly disappeared when they'd decided to end their careers at the brothel. She suspected they had moved far away to get as far from 'Marcos the Enforcer' whom she had not met, but had heard plenty about. Whether he was real or not, she didn't want to know. She also told him of high-stakes poker games that were played there several times a week and she had personally seen tens of thousands of dollars on the poker table.

Samantha had cautioned Brian that possession of all the knowledge she imparted to him could endanger him, and possibly his family. She told him that is why she was hesitant and scared to talk to him, or anyone. She didn't want to go to the police for several reasons. First, she didn't trust them, and second, she was afraid she would be arrested for prostitution. She had never been arrested and didn't want to chance ruining her name.

She was emphatic that many of the city's prominent citizens and leaders were involved, and although she knew a few, she didn't know everyone. She wouldn't give the pastor any names on that night, but said she would think about telling him at a subsequent meeting, if they did meet again. She was very nervous when she divulged the information and she was obviously very scared when she left.

Brian felt a chill come over his body and he shivered uncontrollably for what seemed several minutes. Why did she have to give him all this information? Of all the churches in the phone book, why did she have to pick him? She wasn't part of his flock; she came out of nowhere. He said a silent prayer asking God for protection for him and his family, and for guidance if the whole affair was true. He added a quick prayer for Samantha and all of the other "girls."

Brian was shaken out of his flashback by Ted who came over to the table with a pot of coffee.

"More coffee, Pastor?" he asked.

"Thanks, but I have to go," answered Brian. "I really don't like to be in a bar by myself, doesn't look good, you know."

"I understand. Hope to see ya again sometime. You know, Ralf's isn't just a bar, we're also a family restaurant, so don't be afraid to come in."

"Yes, I've heard that. We'll see," replied Brian getting up to leave.

Ted had heard part of the conversation between the chief and pastor. He couldn't help himself. The bar was empty and they had been the only customers so far that morning.

"Pastor, I don't want you to think I eavesdrop, because I don't. But I couldn't help hearing you talk about a prostitution ring in town." Ted shifted his toothpick to the other side of his mouth as he continued, "I've heard rumors about it too, but I've never said anything to anyone about it."

Brian was shocked by what Ted just told him. He didn't think anyone else knew.

"Where did you hear it?" asked Brian.

"I'm a bartender, Pastor, I hear lots of things. I keep my mouth shut and I don't cause problems. That's the only way I keep my job."

"Okay, I understand. Thanks for the information, Ted, I'm not sure where this will go."

"One bit of caution, Pastor. I don't know how good of friends you are with the chief, or how well you know him, but I wouldn't trust the guy. I've seen too much in the short time I've been here. Just be careful what you say to him."

"Okay, I appreciate the warning."

The caution rang in Brian's head like a giant bell. Why would Ted tell him that? Sure, a bartender hears many rumors; he usually deals with many of the locals who have had more than a few contacts with the chief. Did he know more than he was letting on?

Brian left Ralf's after paying for his coffee and decided to stop at City Hall. He needed to apply for Historic Preservation grant funds to repair the church roof that was starting to lose shingles. The city maintained a line item in its Historic Preservation budget just for churches, but it was on a first come, first serve basis, and there were four historic churches in the city. He desperately needed some of those funds.

Brian parked in front of City Hall and started climbing the multitude of stairs that led to the second floor, where most of the city offices were located. The building had been completely renovated within the past six years with historic funds, as it was built in the 1890s and had been deteriorating badly. The ceilings on each floor were about fifteen feet high, and the climb to the second floor was laborious to most, however Brian was not most people. His workout regime kept him in better shape than people half his age.

He was about halfway up the stairs when he heard a loud voice emanating from the area of the mayor's office.

"He what?" yelled the voice.

Another voice could be heard saying, "Quiet down, he doesn't really know anything. He wasn't sure..." The voice dropped off as he heard a door shut. He couldn't hear the rest of the conversation.

The pastor froze half way up the stairs. He held his breath and pressed himself against the wall, trying to hear more. He was pretty sure the first voice belonged to the Mayor and the second to the police chief, but he wasn't positive. Though the chief did say he was going to see the Mayor.

Brian retreated back down the stairs and out to his car before anyone spotted him. His mind raced as he got into his car and sat behind the steering wheel. What was he going to do now? Who could he turn to? It seemed everyone in authority fell under the description the girl had given him as to who was supposedly involved in this whole fiasco. They were all part of the old time locals, all 'prominent citizens and leaders' as she had stated.

Then it struck Brian like a bolt of lightning. The local newspaper editor was not part of the locals network. Adam Sadowski had come to Cripple Creek about the same time as he had and the editor didn't really socialize with anyone in the good-ole-boys network. He was still considered an outsider. The editorials and articles he had written in his newspaper about the city administration and police department didn't exactly ingratiate Adam to them. He had exposed corruption in prior administrations. He continuously questioned the present administration's decisions.

He would contact Adam, the owner and editor of the Cripple Creek Gazette.

Brian had known Adam for many years and believed him to be a decent sort of guy. He had had many conversations with him in the past and he held his confidence on several occasions. The question was, 'did Adam have any knowledge of what was going on?' He decided he would chew on it for a couple days; there wasn't any big rush to obtain more information.

***

Highway 67, the main highway to Cripple Creek, winds from the town of Divide, 18 miles north of Cripple Creek, to Canon City to the south of Cripple Creek. The ride from Divide is one of the most winding roads found in Colorado with drop-offs from the edge of the road falling hundreds of feet to the valleys below. Part of Highway 67, known locally as Tenderfoot Hill, winds steeply downhill, zigzagging into an old volcanic cauldron known today as the City of Cripple Creek, Colorado.

At the 'scenic view' tourist lookout on the top of Tenderfoot, one can see the entire city in the valley below looking snug and cozy surrounded by mountains and hills on all sides; the Sangre De Cristo mountain range to the south and Pikes Peak to the north. The city sits at an elevation of nine thousand, four hundred, ninety-four feet, almost two miles above sea level, subjecting everyone to the thin, poorly oxygenated air.

CHAPTER 13

He was being chased by a hooded gangster through a trash-filled, dark alley. The long knife the gangster carried shined and reflected in the dim light of the alley. He ran for his life as fast as he could; the alley seemed endless, the night hot and sticky. His legs felt like lead, it was as though he were trying to run through a pool of Jello. Every time he turned to look, the assailant had gained ground on him.

Judge William Tillis awoke with a start. He was sweating profusely and his mouth chalky dry. He threw back the covers to cool off.

He'd been having a nightmare. This had been a recurring for months now, and he couldn't seem to shake it.

Well, the judge thought, *part of the nightmare had some truth to it.*

He glanced over at the shiny new electric wheelchair next to his bed, and then looked out the window across the room. The day had dawned bright and sunny, though the sunshine streaming into the room didn't do anything for his mood.

Life sucked. Bill despised being confined to a wheelchair and damned his bad luck for falling off his roof while re-shingling it two years ago. He had lain there for almost four hours before anyone found him. Many had said he was lucky to have escaped with his life, but he wasn't so sure about that. He didn't consider being paralyzed from the waist down a "blessing."

The judge thought about how fate had really dealt him a miserable, rotten hand. Here he was, the partial owner of a first-class, exclusive brothel with very beautiful women who could give the Pope a boner, and he couldn't even fuck. Why him?

He chuckled to himself. No one could even make up a story that had more lousy luck than that. He thought about the good-ole-days when he used to get free-bees to "test" the brothel's new hires. It was a job he really loved, and as he had told the other partners of 'The Club', "It was something I really got into."

At least, he bragged to himself as a smile lit across his face, I've got the C.D.'s, and no one can take those away from me. He thought about the videos all the time; they were his gold mine. They were insurance; no one in the videos could ever blackmail him. After all, he had the trump cards; he could blackmail many prominent men whenever he so desired. Of course, that would ruin his business, many friendships and probably set him up for a hit. He knew that trump card could only be used as last resort to save his butt.

The judge had so many C.D. recordings; he was going to have to expand his library soon. They barely fit now into his hidden room and if anyone ever found them, he knew his life would be in danger. But for now he felt secure in the knowledge that only he and June knew about them, and she wasn't about to tell anyone.

Tillis always looked forward to Thursday nights. That was the day June always brought him a week's worth of new C.D.'s, and that generally meant at least twenty new recordings for him to watch and enjoy.

Each room in the brothel had a camera hidden placed in an ornate wall sconce. They were so tiny that unless you knew where they were, you would never find them. The cameras also picked up all conversations and noises with highly sensitive built-in microphones. The taping system for all the rooms was in a cabinet in June's office, which she always kept under lock and key.

William and June always had dinner at his place and enjoyed a bottle of wine on Thursday nights. Her company was always a pleasure and he derived great joy in flaunting his culinary talents to create a special dish each week. They would talk about the business and discuss different problems and solutions, and would often discuss local and national politics as well. June was well versed in the political climate at all levels. Conversation with her was always entertaining, but not nearly as entertaining as the disks.

Right after June left, William would spend the rest of the night cataloging and enjoying *his* new C.D.'s, filing them away and notating in his logbook as to who was in them and their specific sexual tastes and desires. He would often grade the interlude, with separate scores for the customer and the employee.

He especially liked watching Blaze and China Doll. To him, they were the most stunning and exotic women in the world. As he watched transfixed, they performed their magic on customers and he imagined himself as their clients. It was like watching a beautiful, delicate dance; a waltz, which was perfect in every step of its predisposed ending.

***

The judge pulled himself into his wheelchair and headed for the bathroom. It was time for him to get ready for another unfulfilling day.

It was a Wednesday. On Wednesdays, Judge Tillis held court in Cripple Creek for infractions of the city's ordinances. Most of his cases were comprised of barking or loose dogs, parking infractions, speeding, and stop sign violations. Juveniles before him were usually there for skateboarding on the sidewalks, underage smoking, possession of beer or other alcoholic beverages, drugs or curfew violations. Fines or convictions in his court were strictly local matters. They were never forwarded to any state or federal databases for any permanent record. Most of his punishments consisted of either fines or community service. It usually depended on the number of previous violations, and most of all, how the offender addressed the Court and the Judge.

He was occasionally asked to 'take care' of an infraction or two by special interests in the city, or by the chief. The judge could always be depended upon to oblige the special requests.

***

In its heyday, the Old Homestead House was probably the most prosperous and expensive

brothel in Cripple Creek. Known as Cripple Creek's "soiled dove," Pearl de Vere operated the historic Homestead House on Myers Ave., catering only to the most prosperous and wealthy men.

The above photograph is believed to be, but cannot be confirmed, the only existing photo of Pearl de Vere. Described as slender and beautiful, with flaming red hair, there are no confirmed photos. She died in 1897 of a suspected morphine overdose and was the only known prostitute allowed burial in Mt. Pisgah cemetery.

It was reported that she had the largest funeral procession that Cripple Creek had ever seen.

Photo is courtesy of The Old Homestead House Museum and is believed to be Pearl de Vere.

The Homestead House is one of the last historic original brothel museums in Colorado. It is located on Myers Ave in Cripple Creek and is open to the public. Call ahead for hours.

CHAPTER 14

Brian stopped by the newspaper office early Monday morning. He figured Adam would be at his computer busily typing away and laying out the newspaper for the weekly run. As he entered the two-story wood frame office, Adam's wife, Linda, greeted him and they exchanged a few pleasantries.

"Is Adam available this morning?" he asked with a wink. "Or is he too busy coming down on the poor politicians of Cripple Creek again?"

"He's upstairs working on the ads for the week," she replied with a smile. "I think he would take a break. Would you like me to get him?"

"Would you ask him if he could tear himself away for few minutes?" inquired Brian. Linda went upstairs and came back down with Adam trailing her.

"Hey, Brian, what brings you here today?" asked Adam.

"Let's take a walk," Brian replied. He then turned to Linda, "Would you mind if I steal your husband for a couple of minutes?"

"Only a couple?" Linda queried with an impish smile, "Keep him all day if you want, I don't need him. He's just in the way."

"Maybe I will," Brian said to Linda who was amused by her own jabs at her husband.

"OK, but let me get my cell phone. I'm expecting a call from the Mayor and it's hard enough to get him to call me back, and I don't want to miss him. If he calls I may have to excuse myself for a couple minutes to speak with him," said Adam.

"That's alright. There's no hurry, I've got lots of time today," Brian replied.

"I wish I did," Adam replied as he dashed upstairs and returned with his cell phone. They both left the building and started walking down the cement sidewalk towards town.

Brian was quiet, momentarily wondering if what he was about to ask Adam was going to backfire on him.

"What's up?" asked Adam nonchalantly.

"Adam," Brian started hesitantly, "I've been told what I am about to ask you could be dangerous. I'm in uncharted territory here and I'm very hesitant to talk to anyone about it, but..., have you ever heard anything about a brothel or prostitution ring here in town?"

Adam stopped in his tracks and faced Brian directly. "Where did that come from?" he questioned. The blood seemed to have drained from his face.

Brian studied tried to study Adam's face. The eyes were the road to the soul he thought, and he still needed to know if Adam was involved. He was obviously shaken by the question; so much so, Brian wondered if he should end this now and return home.

"You know I can't tell you that. Just suffice that I came upon the information and I was told it could be harmful to my family and myself just to know about it. I figure I am taking a big risk just by talking to you, but I hope I know you well enough that you aren't involved and you will keep my confidentiality. Please tell me you are not involved. Please tell me."

***

They continued walking down the street while Adam thought about how he could or should respond. He could tell Brian was nervous, almost ready to turn back.

"I can't answer your first question just now. And no, I'm not involved, but I have heard about it. And, yes, I'll definitely keep your confidence."

Adam turned and looked down at the sidewalk.

"Just please don't ask me anymore questions about this right now. I'll have to get back to you. I can tell you and assure you, though, that I am on the outside looking in, just as you are, and your trust in me isn't misplaced. I just can't say anything more to you at this point."

*****

The answer shocked and surprised Brian. He wasn't expecting anything like what he'd just heard.

"Does that also include the high-stakes poker games?" he inquired not thinking he was asking too much.

Adam just looked at Brian, revealing nothing. It was obvious he wasn't going to say anything more, and Adam's demeanor seemed to implore Brian for understanding. This piqued Brian's curiosity even more about what he didn't know, and what Adam did.

"I think I should tell you that I also had a conversation with the police chief about this. I spoke to him at Ralf's. The bartender, Ted, overheard some of our conversation, came to me later and told me he also had heard whispers of what we discussed."

"And…?"

"And, I really believe the chief acted kind of nervous when I asked him the same questions I asked you. He all of a sudden remembered he had an appointment with the Mayor supposedly about some parking issues and he had to run off. The whole thing was all sort of weird," Brian related to Adam.

"What do you mean, weird?" asked Adam.

"Well, I had to go to City Hall a little bit later to see the Planning and Historic Preservation Director about some historic funds to help repair the church roof. As I was climbing the stairs I overheard the chief talking with the Mayor in his office. It sounded like the Mayor was kind of upset when the chief talked to him. I didn't exactly hear what was said, but I heard enough to be pretty sure the chief was telling the Mayor about meeting with me."

"Brian," pleaded Adam, "Please don't talk to anyone else about this. You may have said too much to too many people already."

"All right Adam, I won't ask you any more questions. I hope you do get back to me though, and soon. I'm really starting to worry about the safety of my family. When do you think that will happen?"

Adam just shrugged his shoulders, "I can't say when, but I'll make it a priority. I have to make a phone call. I'll talk to you soon though, have a good day." He shook Brian's hand, and abruptly turned around and headed back to his office.

Brian stood looking at Adam as he walked back down the street. He was trying to take in and figure out what Adam had just told him; trying to read between the lines. Although Adam had not said much, Brian realized that what wasn't said was probably just as important. Why would he have to get back to him? Why couldn't he talk to him now? Who did he have to call?

It was obvious he was going to talk to someone about the conversation they had just had, but to whom? If what Adam had said that Brian's trust wasn't misplaced, and Adam wasn't lying, then either the newspaper was doing an undercover investigation or it must be a law enforcement agency he is talking to; but which one? Local-no way. County, slightly possible.

State, most probable. Federal? No way, they wouldn't give a care about local prostitutes or illegal poker games.

If Adam was lying to him, and he was actually part of the ring of those responsible for the prostitution and gambling activity, then Brian knew he opened up a can of worms and he and his family may be in imminent danger. He may have to start watching over his shoulder and even tell his wife what was going on.

Could he trust Adam? Should he send his family away until he figured this out? He didn't know which scenario was valid, and that presented the real quandary for him. But, he figured, there was nothing he could do right now anyway, he was basically in the dark. All he could do was wait and trust that Adam was telling him the truth.

***

Numerous Victorian and small cabin-size homes dot the landscape, many built in the late 1800s during Cripple Creek's glorious gold rush heydays. Many of the homes built in recent years were designed to blend in with and compliment the existing structures. Any new homes built in the city were encouraged to be historic looking.

At the turn of the 19th century, Cripple Creek was a bustling metropolis having upwards of forty to fifty thousand inhabitants thanks to its thriving gold mining industry. Colorado's who's who at the time considered designating Cripple Creek the state capitol.

CHAPTER 15

Several days had passed since Pastor Brian had spoken with Adam and he was getting very uneasy. A queasy feeling was constant in his gut; he couldn't sleep. Adam had told him he would get back to him soon. Brian had taken that to mean *real* soon. He hadn't talked to anyone else about the information, per Adam's instructions, and he still wasn't positive Adam was the one he should have been confiding in about it either. He silently reprimanded himself for being so trusting; maybe way too trusting. He thought maybe he should have gone to the State level in order to be sure he was talking to someone not involved in this whole affair. He'd go to the FBI if he could, but he knew there was no federal crime here; just prostitution and gambling, all state misdemeanors, and even the Colorado Bureau of Investigation may not even be interested in such local problems. But why would his life, and that of his family, be threatened for such a small infraction of the law? He couldn't figure it out. There had to be something much larger he couldn't see.

***

The phone rang at the pastor's house and his wife answered. He heard her converse in the next room for a moment before bringing the phone to him in the den.

"It's Adam, he wants to speak to you," stated Christine handing Brian the phone. She was unaware that he had been waiting for Adam's call.

"Hello, Adam," Brian quickly said, "about time!"

"Yeah, I know; we need to talk. I figure you probably know what it's about. I have some information for you that you need to know about. When are you free?"

"I can be free just about anytime; do you mean now?"

"If you can. Where can we meet?"

Brian thought for a moment. He didn't want to go to Ralf's again, there wasn't much privacy there. "How about the church office, would you be okay with that?" he asked.

"That'll be fine. I'm coming for my guidance counseling." Adam laughed. "Make sure no one else is around though," Adam said sounding more serious. "We have to be alone."

"Okay, give me a few minutes to turn the lights and the heat on. I'll see you there in about fifteen."

"What's up with Adam?" asked Christine.

Brian hesitated. "Please don't ask me anything about this, Hon. I can't talk about it right now."

Christine had a puzzled look, but she knew better than to ask anymore.

***

About twenty minutes later Adam walked through the church's front door and into Brian's office located off to the left of the vestibule. He looked around as if he was checking to make sure they were alone.

"Hey, Adam," Brian stated as he held out his hand. "I was just wondering before you called me when I would be hearing from you again."

"Are we alone?" Adam questioned, wanting to be sure.

"We are," stated Brian, getting up to shut the door. "The room is soundproof, for counseling purposes, you know," he said smiling, referring to Adam's prior remark on the phone.

Adam took a seat in front of Brian's desk.

"Brian," Adam stated, "As I told you before, this is very serious. I need you to promise that you won't breathe a word to anyone of what I am about to tell you. There can be no mistakes, no slip of the tongue or slip-ups. This time I need *your* trust."

"You have my word, you know that."

"I know, but I have to make sure that you thoroughly understand how serious this is before I tell you anything. Those are my instructions."

"Instructions?" questioned Brian, "From whom? What do you mean?" He could hardly contain his curiosity now.

"Hold on, Brian, slow down. I'm afraid you've stumbled big time into an ongoing FBI investigation."

"FBI?"

"Yes, I've been told there are much larger things going on here that even I don't know about, but even I can't ask too many questions. Besides, even if I did, they probably wouldn't give me any answers anyway."

"What kind of investigation?" Brian was now intrigued.

"Hold on, hold on, I'm getting to it," Adam responded smiling.

"First, my contact at the FBI asked me if I could rely on you to keep this under your hat and keep your mouth shut. I told him I could. I stuck my neck out here, Brian, and I hope I'm not going to get it cut off. Next, I was told to tell you specific things, which I am going to relate to you in a minute, and then, third, they have a request of you."

"A request of me?"

Adam continued, "Yes. The FBI has information that a brothel has been operating somewhere in Cripple Creek for sometime now, but they don't really give a flying shit about the prostitution. Excuse my French.

They are aware of the poker games also, and don't care about that either. But what they still need is the location, or who owns it or runs it. They have ideas, and possibilities, but they don't know for sure and they can't risk tipping anyone off. They have other reasons for wanting the information, which even I don't know anything about."

"So what do they want of me?" Brian asked.

"I'm getting to that," Adam replied. "Several months ago the FBI came to me and asked me to let them know if I ever hear anything in town about a brothel or the high-stakes poker games. I had never heard anything about them before they briefed me. I asked them why they came to me and they said since I was the editor of the newspaper they thought I would hear things others may not. Besides, they said before contacting me, they did a background check, and found I had once held a top secret special intelligence clearance working with NSA, so I guess they kind of figured that I could keep a secret."

"NSA?" asked Brian.

"National Security Agency. I was an analyst there many, many years ago, and had a top secret crypto clearance and access."

"I didn't know that about you, Adam, I'm impressed," Brian said with a broad grin.

Adam smiled and continued, "There's probably a lot of things you don't know about me; we won't go any farther on that. Anyway, they told me about the investigation and gave me a number of an agent to contact if I ever thought I saw or heard anything relating to the prostitution or poker. That is why I couldn't answer you when you asked me those questions. I had to make the call first. That was the first time I had heard anything about it. You surprised me and it kind of shook me up."

Adam laughed. He was suddenly embarrassed by the admission he had just made to Brian that he was shook up.

"You, shook up?"

"So, along comes little 'ole Brian, the pastor of a local church, asking me questions about a bunch of prostitutes, brothels and poker games. Yeah, it kind of set me back on my heels for a few, it had me thinking."

Brian had to laugh too. It was funny, he thought, putting it that way.

"OK, so what now?" asked Brian.

"This is where we're at," said Adam looking down at the floor while tying to think of how to ask Brian to do what the FBI wanted him to do. "It's kind of complicated, so follow me on this. You told me the chief was nervous when you spoke to him. Then you believed the Mayor flipped out in his office when the chief told the Mayor what you told him. Based on this, the FBI believes both may possibly be involved. But they need to know where the brothel is located and they haven't been able to find that out. They believe the Mayor might be the weak link, he might be the first to crack if any pressure is put on him."

"So why don't they haul him in, put the pressure on him and make him crack?"

"They would, except if he doesn't crack, the whole operation may get shut down and that's what they *don't* want. They would like for you to go ask him the same questions that you asked the police chief and me. Tell him you have information about the brothel and poker games; that you talked to the police chief and he blew you off but you believe it exists, that it's real, and you would like to see an investigation. They want to monitor his response, what he'll do, where he'll go, who he'll talk to."

"You mean they want me to wear a wire?" asked Brian.

"No, no," responded Adam. "They just want to watch him for a day or so after you tell him, so they can see where he goes and who he talks to."

Brian thought for a moment. "You're the newspaper editor, why don't *you* go ask the Mayor those questions?"

"Think about it, Brian. They already know that you have some knowledge of the existence of the place, although they don't know how much knowledge you have. Now, if I go in and start asking questions, they may get real nervous and shut it down. As I told you, the FBI doesn't want that to happen yet."

"Let me think about this one, Adam. This is kind of strange. Can I get back to *you* this time?"

"Definitely," Adam said with a wink. How soon will that be?"

"Soon," he stated smiling.

***

They shook hands again, and Adam saw himself out of the church while Brian sat down at his desk to think for a while. What Adam had told him was much more than he had ever imagined he would hear. Now the FBI wanted him to get involved, to take an active part in the investigation. How did this come about? Why in the hell did he have to ask Adam anything in the first place? Why did Samantha have to come to him and tell him what she did? The questions kept replaying in his head, over and over again.

Brian went into the church, knelt down before the alter and prayed. He didn't know what to do. He wanted to rid the town of any prostitution, sins of the flesh, and illegal poker, but at the same time he was a man of God, not a cop or investigator. People needed to trust that if they talked to him, it would always be in confidence. He could not break that trust unless under extreme circumstances.

Tomorrow, he must tell Adam to let the FBI know he could not do what they wanted. He would have to tell him *no*.

***

When Brian arose the next day, he felt good about his decision to turn down the request by the FBI. He called Adam and asked him to meet him again at his office, which he agreed to. He would be there in half an hour.

Adam arrived right on time. Brian closed the door and sat down at his desk. "I'm sorry, Adam, but I can't do it. I can't be a pastor and play undercover cop at the same time."

Adam smiled, "It's all right, the FBI had expected that exact decision; but they had to try. I guess the job falls to me now."

"What do you mean?" asked Brian, surprised at the statement.

"I told them I would talk to the Mayor if you didn't," replied Adam, "so I need to go over some things with you. I'm going in to the Mayor's office as an investigative reporter. I'm going to tell him that I had a conversation with you and ask him basically the same questions that you asked the police chief. He, I'm sure, will deny any knowledge, and, if I know him, he'll try to hurry me out of his office. This is where I'll have a little fun insisting that he investigate the information thoroughly. We'll see what happens."

Brian could see that Adam had no problem performing the task asked by the FBI. As a matter of fact, it looked like he was going to enjoy it. Brian secretly wished he could have gone to see the Mayor, ask him all the questions and watch him squirm, but knew he was now out of it.

"So what is it you need to go over with me?" inquired Brian.

"If anyone ever asks, I'm going to say I got the information from you asking me the same questions you asked the chief. It's the truth, so I figured you wouldn't have a real problem with anything like that. It's just to cover me, and you, and the story that I give the Mayor, that's all. Then hopefully you'll be out of it and all finished with the whole thing. Hopefully it'll also take any heat off of you."

Brian chewed on his lower lip as he contemplated Adam's request. Finally, he sighed and agreed to what Adam had asked.

"Tell me Adam, why did you agree to do this?"

Adam laughed. "Are you kidding? This could be huge! This could be a major story when it's all said and done, and I'll have the scoop on the whole thing. That was the promise to me. If there is nothing to the story, no harm, no foul. I've just got a feeling this is going to be all true and be a very big story. I could make the AP and Reuters, maybe even CNN and FOX."

Brian chuckled. He was relieved that Adam wasn't mad at him and that the investigation was going to continue without him. He felt as though a huge weight had been lifted off his shoulders.

As Adam was leaving, he turned to Brian, "Have you happened to notice the guy down the street sitting in a black car? Couldn't make out much as I passed him, but he's a pretty big guy with a large beard. I've seen the car there a couple times the past few days. Don't know who he is and I don't want to make you nervous, but be careful and watch your back. Keep your doors locked for a couple days until I talk to the Mayor. That'll take any heat off you."

"Thanks for the heads up, Adam. Let me know when you have the conversation."

"Will do."

***

As with any large city, and particularly a mining city, Cripple Creek's economy of yesteryear included a number of not so desirous enterprises including casinos, dancehalls, and taverns; one unsavory type in particular being the parlour houses, the local houses of prostitution. They lined Cripple Creek's red light district on Myers Avenue south of town where ladies of the night plied their trade. The 'proper' ladies avoided the area at all costs.

There were a few fancy parlour houses and many other one room tents or shacks known as cribs. The parlour houses were run by Madams and had stables of young, beautiful girls available for pleasure-for the right price.

CHAPTER 16

Pastor Brian was relieved on one hand, but nervous about his family's safety on the other. He knew he was no longer involved in the whole affair anymore, but he still had to be careful until Adam had the conversation with the Mayor. He was having supper with his wife and daughter when the phone rang.

"I'll get it," said Brian pushing his chair out from the table.

"Why don't you sit down and finish dinner first," grumbled his wife. "If it's important, they'll leave a message."

Brain hesitated and then said, "Let me get it." He picked up the cordless phone.

"Hello, Pastor Brian speaking."

"Hello, Pastor, this is Chief Campbell. I've got some news for you."

"Hello, Chief. Listen, can I call you back? I'm eating supper right now," Brian stated, looking over at his wife who was glaring her disapproval, giving him 'the look'."

"Look, I wanted to give you an update; my men and the gaming investigators made a couple of arrests of prostitutes last night in a casino. That's all, just wanted you to know," the chief stated in a hurry.

"OK. Great. I'll talk to you later about it," said Brian, looking over at his wife.

Brian went back to the supper table and sat down.

"Who and what was that all about?" queried Christine.

"I'll have to tell you about it later," replied Brian darting his eyes toward their daughter. Christine immediately caught on and didn't ask any more questions.

Brian thought about the telephone conversation. It seemed a little strange that the chief would call him to tell him about the arrests. Were they at a place under a casino? He hadn't told the chief about that part of the information, he had held that back. The more he thought about it, the stranger it seemed.

Brian also wondered what he was going to tell his wife. He had thought it was okay to ask the chief and Adam about the brothel; they didn't know who had given him the information. But his wife, she would know, and that presented another dilemma. It was beginning to look like he wasn't done with this quagmire after all.

After supper, Brian helped his wife and daughter clear the dishes and clean up. He told his wife he had to go down to the office for a few minutes to return the chief's call, and he would be back soon.

Brian casually walked the distance to the church, keeping an eye out for the black car. He arrived at the church, unlocked the door to his office and sat down at his desk. He dialed the chief's number.

"Chief Campbell," came the answer on the phone.

"Chief, this is Pastor Brian. Sorry I couldn't talk earlier. I was eating supper and my wife and daughter were close by. They know nothing of what I discussed with you."

"That's okay, Brian, I just wanted to let you know we arrested two hookers that I guess have been working the casinos for a few weeks. Hopefully, they were the ones you told me about and it takes care of the situation."

"Where were they arrested, Chief?" asked Brian.

The question temporarily took the chief by surprise and he hesitated, answering, "Why, I haven't read the officer's report yet; let me look real quick." The chief was stumbling for an answer. "Says here in the report they were arrested at the Miner's Claim Casino."

"Okay, great, Chief, good job," Brian stated, wanting the chief to feel like he was patting him on the back. "Now all we need to find is the high-stakes poker game."

Brian knew the arrests were not part of the prostitution ring they had discussed. The girls in the prostitution ring were not street hookers, they were high-priced women working at what Samantha called a high-class brothel. Also, Brian knew the Miner's Claim Casino was small and had no room for a poker table, let alone some high-stakes poker games and a brothel, unless there were secret areas he did not know about. He knew something really smelled about this whole conversation.

He said goodbye to the chief and sat at his desk going over the conversation in his mind. He also remembered Samantha warning him about the 'prominent citizens and leaders' of the community being involved. Although there was nothing concrete that pointed to him, it was beginning to look like the chief may be involved.

Brian weighed his options. He could forget about what just occurred, or call Adam and let him know so he could call the FBI and fill them in. He decided on the latter. If the chief truly was involved in this racket, Adam and the FBI had to know. They would be the only ones that could actually find out.

Brian called Adam at home.

"Hello, Sadowski residence," Adam answered.

"Adam, this is Brian, I have to talk to you. There have been some developments I think you ought to know about."

"Brian, can it wait till tomorrow? I was just going out to dinner with my wife."

"It'll only take a minute, but I think you'll want to know. It's about you-know-what," returned Brian. "But it can wait if you don't have time."

"Hold on. Give me a moment," said Adam.

He heard Adam se the phone down.

He came back and said, "I'll see you in the morning. I'll call you first thing."

Brian agreed and told Adam to give him a call around ten if that was convenient for him.

The pastor locked up the church and headed home. He was thinking about what he was going to tell his wife. She deserved to know why he was acting like he was, making all the phone calls, going to confidential meetings, but at the same time she would probably tie the activity back to Samantha.

When Brian arrived home, Christine was just putting Madison to bed. This would be a good time to talk to his wife he thought. As Christine returned, he sat down at the kitchen table.

"I'm going to make some hot chocolate, want some?" Christine asked.

"That would be great."

As she prepared the hot chocolate, Brian started explaining his situation. "Hon, I know some things have been kind of strange lately, but I'm going to ask you not to ask me any questions about what is going on right now. I may be able to tell you about it or tell you *some* things later on, but I just can't right now without violating my confidentiality with the lady who came to see me. I hope you understand."

Christine didn't know Samantha's name, she just remembered her as the woman with the bright red hair. He continued, "I can talk to others some of what was discussed between me and the woman, but they have no idea where the information came from, and I just tell them I came upon some information. So you see, if I told you anything, you would know what we had talked about, and that wouldn't be right. It would violate the confidentiality she expected."

Christine knew what Brian was saying, "I understand, dear. I just wish it wouldn't interfere with supper and our other family times together."

Brian realized where Christine was coming from also, and he wished he could tell her more so she would identify with what he felt he had to do and when. Things were difficult enough, he thought, without having family problems over it also.

***

The next morning Brian was working in the garden when the call came in from Adam. He asked Brian if they could meet somewhere besides Brian's office. He thought people might get suspicious if they saw him going to his church during the day too often, especially since Adam wasn't a church-going kind of guy. Brian agreed to go to Adam's office this time. He told his wife where he was going; he would be back shortly, and left for the short walk to Adam's.

When Brian arrived at Adam's office, Adam was outside smoking a cigarette as Colorado had recently passed laws against smoking in any business place the public had access to.

"Morning, Pastor, how's things this morning?"

"Great," Brian responded.

"Let's go on in up to my office," Adam said. "We'll have some privacy for a few minutes till my wife gets back from the post office."

They climbed the steep, narrow stairway to Adam's cramped office. To the uninitiated, the office appeared to be somewhere in between a mess and organized. It was an organized mess. Although things seemed scattered all over, Adam could place his hands on any document he wanted. The large computer screen scrolling pictures of his family dominated his desktop.

"Whatcha got?" Adam asked.

Brian told Adam about the phone call from Reggie, the police chief. "I have a feeling he was calling me to make me feel the prostitution thing was solved, to keep me from wondering about it any more," related Brian. "The whole thing seemed funny. He didn't even know where the women were arrested. It was as though he was shocked that I asked the question."

"I'll do a little checking, see what I can find out." said Adam. "Let me make a phone call, I have some contacts at the Teller County Sheriff's Department in Divide. The women would have had to be transported there by the Cripple Creek Police Department after they were arrested. I'll see if I can get some names, that should be public information."

"I'm also going to interview the Mayor today," Adam said with a sly smile, "I have an appointment at noon. It should be a real interesting meeting."

"I'll say," agreed Brian with a wide grin, "I wish I could be a fly on the wall. It doesn't bother me to be out of this though. It's starting to wear on my family and me. Hopefully this will be it for me. I'll catch you later, Adam, I've got to get back home."

"Sure, Thanks for coming by."

Adam picked up the phone and dialed his friend at the Sheriff's department. Every good reporter has contacts at different levels of law enforcement in their coverage area, and Adam was no different. He had done some favors for the different departments before and they were not averse to helping him once in a while with a little inside information. He had never abused the arrangement and had developed a close working relationship. This request would just be an early report that was available to all press agencies. No big deal.

His contact at the Sheriff's Department happened to be working when Adam called.

"Hey, Frankie, Adam Sadowski, got a minute?"

"Well, long time no hear, what can I do ya for?" Frankie bellowed. Frankie was a cheerful guy; he never seemed to have a bad day.

He checked the arrest logs and reported back to Adam. "Nothing, Adam, no females brought in last night for prostitution."

"Can you double check, this is really important?"

"Sure, but I know it's going to be the same answer."

"How about the day before or today?" Adam asked. The answer was still negative. Adam was told they hadn't had any females brought in under arrest in a couple days.

This didn't present a dilemma to Adam, he thought, but it was going to be a problem for the chief.

"Thanks for the info, Frankie. I'll fill you in when I know more, but for now could ya keep this inquiry under your hat?"

"You got it, Adam; happy to help. Let me know if there's anything else you need."

Adam thanked the deputy and told him he would brief him on what it was all about sometime in the future, but for now he asked that the deputy keep their conversation confidential.

Adam leaned back in his chair and smiled as he thought about how Brian would react when he told him what he had discovered. Brian sounded like he desperately wanted out of the whole situation, so maybe he wouldn't tell him. He would have to think about it. Meanwhile, Adam knew he would have to call his FBI contact in Denver. Even though they could prove everything the chief told Brian was a lie, it didn't prove anything in and of itself; but he was sure the FBI would find the whole incident interesting and maybe it would

tie in with something else they knew about. He decided
to wait until after the meeting with the Mayor to call.

***

*The small cribs were generally a one-woman
show; either a former prostitute from a brothel
who was now diseased or disfigured, or an older
woman beyond her "prime" plying the only trade
she knew.*

*The more expensive and eloquent parlour
houses would charge upwards of two hundred and
fifty dollars per night, but would usually include a
lavish meal and any liquors of choice. A crib, on
the other hand, may only charge twenty-five cents
for a basic, quick 'trick', where the men usually
kept their boots on.*

CHAPTER 17

It was a warm, breezy, sunny day, and Adam decided to walk the half-mile down Bennett Avenue to City Hall. He could see storm clouds to the west, and he thought how apropos this was to what the Mayor was going to experience in a few minutes. He gathered his thoughts on how he was going to approach the Mayor and ask the questions the FBI needed answers to.

It was five minutes till noon when Adam arrived at City Hall and climbed the stairs to the second floor where the Mayor's office was located. He went into the office where the Mayor's secretary, Eileen, sat behind her desk. She was on the phone, but looked up and acknowledged Adam with a nod of her head. She put the caller on hold. "Can I get you a cup of coffee, Adam?"

"That's okay, I'll get it myself," Adam offered as he headed toward the coffee pot and poured some into a Styrofoam cup, adding a little non-dairy creamer to lighten it up.

"He's expecting you, Adam, let me see if he's ready," she told him as she walked over to a door and knocked.

"Enter," came a voice from the office.

"Dan, Adam is here."

"Show him in."

Adam walked into the office and Eileen closed the door behind him.

"Hello Adam, how are you doing today?" asked Mayor Daniel Comeau getting up from behind his desk and extending his hand to Adam.

Adam knew the Mayor didn't really care how well he was; hell, he was a politician and he knew he had to a least act like he cared. They had gone head to head before, but both had always maintained a professional relationship.

"Just fine, just fine," Adam responded

.

***

"So, what brings you here today?" asked the Mayor. He really hated talking to Adam in one-on-one meetings like this. Adam had previously printed some exposé's of unprofessional activities in the administration that resulted in, at a minimum, embarrassment for the city and the Mayor, and a few city employees being terminated. He was determined not to let Adam get the upper hand today. He knew of nothing going on in the city that would cause him any embarrassment, or so he thought.

Adam knew the Mayor and wanted to relax him first before he hit him with any of the big questions. The Mayor was always edgy when Adam asked his first questions, as the Mayor didn't know what he was up to yet or the subjects he would broach.

"Mr. Mayor," started Adam, "it's getting downright dark in town, almost half the streetlights are burned out on Bennett Avenue and they continue to burn out one by one. They haven't been replaced in almost six months now. How come?"

The Mayor relaxed as he sat back in his seat and lifted his arms, cradling the back of his head in his intertwined fingers. The editor already knew the answer, but now he was going to have a little fun.

"Adam, you know we've been working on that for months now. It's a contract dispute we have with the power company we use to replace and service them. We had a meeting with them last week and have just reached an agreement. I was told all the burned out lights in town will be replaced by the end of the month."

The Mayor was feeling confident now.

"I thought that was what you were going to say, Dan, but I had to ask. How about the new City Hall, how is it coming?" Adam was playing with the Mayor, he knew the new City Hall, of which even the construction was a very controversial subject, and had a long way to go. There had been embarrassing missteps in the design and construction, which had caused many delays. Adam had covered them all in the newspaper, and he knew the building was a sore spot with the Mayor, but it wouldn't put him on edge. The Mayor had answered countless questions about it to so many residents and reporters, that he had pretty much come up with pat answers.

"It's coming along, Adam, they put the new elevator shaft in this week, then the roof ought to be on by the end of the month," stated the Mayor, obviously bored with the question.

Adam thought the Mayor was pretty much disarmed by now, as he was relaxed in his chair sipping on his coffee. He thought it was time to spring the FBI's questions on him.

"Well," Adam continued smiling inwardly, "I've been hearing rumors around about a prostitution ring and some high-stakes poker games that are supposedly taking place in town. Can you enlighten me or do you know anything about any of it?"

***

The Mayor stared into his coffee cup trying to collect his thoughts. *Oh shit,* he thought to himself, *he's been talking to the pastor.* He put his coffee down, sat upright in his chair and pulled himself to his desk.

"Well, from what I hear, the police arrested a couple of hookers last night. That's unusual around here, but not unheard of," the Mayor said coughing intermittently. He was doing everything he could not to look at Adam, sipping his coffee several times.

***

Adam had him just where he wanted him. The Mayor gave the exact answer he thought he was going to give.

I wonder if I should say anything about the Sheriff's Department not booking any of the prostitutes into the jail? They had to be brought there if they were arrested, to be processed; that was the procedure. The only reason they probably wouldn't have been booked into the county jail is if the chief had let them go, maybe to be two more in his long list of informants. But then, Adam thought, why would he even tell anyone he had arrested them?

"I don't know, Dan, they don't seem to fit the information I received, but I'll talk to the chief and see if I can get their names. I'm still wondering how he caught them; I'd like to hear about that. It'd make a good story. Have you heard anything about the high-stakes poker games?" Adam asked without missing a beat. He was relishing the fun he was having and the angst the Mayor continued to have. He could hardly contain himself.

The Mayor's face was flushed now. Adam wondered if it was from the coughing or if he was mad enough to spit nails. The mayor wanted this interview over, and quickly.

"Haven't heard a thing," he told Adam. He was having a coughing fit now, and got up to walk around his office.

"Are you alright, Dan?" Adam was delighting in the Mayor's nervousness and false confidence.

"I'm fine," he responded, "Anything else?"

Adam figured he had put him through enough for now. "That's all I have for now, Dan. I'll follow up with you later." Adam got up and stretched his arms.

Adam shook the Mayor's hand and turned around to leave, but hesitated in the doorway. "Get that cough looked at, Dan."

Adam was ecstatic. Now he was going to have to call the FBI and update them on Brian's episode with the police chief and his meeting with the Mayor.

***

A daily wage for most miners at the time was three dollars. They could not afford the eloquent parlour houses; those were reserved for the affluent men of money, the millionaires, the men of wealth and status.

CHAPTER 18

After the Mayor's interview with Adam, Dan was visibly upset. His hands were shaking. He paced the floor in his office for several minutes.

"Eileen, please cancel the remainder of my meetings today, I have a monster headache. I'll be at home if there are any emergencies."

The Mayor went to his car and headed for the nearest liquor store, and bought a fifth of Johnny Walker Black Label Scotch before going home. That was his favorite drink, and he needed something stiff right now to calm his nerves. The editor was asking too many questions, ones that he didn't particularly like.

Dan unlocked the door to his house and slipped inside, clutching his bottle of scotch. He re-locked the door, grabbed three clear rocks glasses with ice and carried them to the living room, along with the bottle of scotch.

He poured a double into each glass and placed a drink before each of his guests seated on the black Naugahyde couch. They were dressed for dinner. The man wore a dinner jacket, white shirt and black slacks and black leather shoes. The woman was dressed in a knee skimming red halter dress, silver braided neck chain and silver platform shoes. Dan kept a glass for himself and started rambling about his day to his seated relatives.

"God damn it, I told you I shouldn't have got into this. But noooo, you told me it would be a good investment." He took another drink. "I shouldn't have listened to you."

His company didn't move or comment, nor did they touch their drinks, they just sat staring off into space while Dan continued his tirade and gulped down his scotch.

The Mayor brought his guests out of the closet whenever he felt the need for a sounding board. They had been shut up in there for three long years now. After he'd completed detox he felt he could function just fine in simple society without them. He hadn't needed them for a long time. But now it was different. Dan was so alone and confused, and couldn't talk to anyone else- they'd judge him or talk back. He didn't need that kind of pressure, he just needed someone to listen.

June listened to him, but at times she could be very judgmental.

Uncle Peter and Auntie Ethel weren't like that; they loved him and would never demean him. When he saw that they weren't interested in their scotch, he allowed himself to consume their beverages, then refilled their glasses in case they changed their minds and became thirsty.

The mannequins were always polite and very well dressed. Dan took pride in making them presentable for each other and himself. Uncle Peter and Auntie Ethel had left behind closets full of clothing when they passed away. Dan used those clothes to dress his mannequin relatives for various occasions. They were great company.

The Mayor wanted out. He didn't have the stomach or the nerves for this kind of pressure, and now didn't even know why he got involved in 'The Club' in the first place. It all sounded exciting when it started. They had made quite a bit of money, but it quickly became very serious. People got hurt.

Now townsfolk were asking questions. Not just the editor, but the pastor also. The Mayor's paranoia and heightened anxiety had him believing that everyone was talking about 'The Club'. They were all looking at him; he could feel their eyes on him. They were staring at him; they were talking about him.

***

Dan had consumed several drinks by the time he called Reggie on his cell phone. The chief answered right away, when he saw it was the Mayor's home number on the digital display.

"Good Afternoon, Dan, what can I do for you?" asked the chief.

"I want out," blurted Dan.

Reggie could detect some slurring of his words. "What the hell are you doing? You know better that to call me on my cell. Are you drunk, you son of a bitch?" the chief yelled at Dan.

"I'm sorry, Chief. Call me at my home," said Dan slowly slurring every word.

The chief hung up and called the Mayor back from a landline phone.

"What do you mean, you want out? No one has asked to get out before. Even if they let you out, you'll probably lose all your investment. Do you want that? That's a lot of money to throw away."

The chief was silent for a moment, and then asked, "What brought this on? You're drinking again, aren't you?"

"They're all talking about us, Reggie, they're all talking about us. They're watching us, too. I want out. I don't care what it costs me," slurred Dan.

The chief knew he couldn't talk to the Mayor when he was drunk. He had been sober for almost three years, now he had to deal with a drunk again.

"I'll talk to you tomorrow, Dan, when you're sober. I'll meet you and June for breakfast," the chief said wanting to end the conversation.

"OK, Reggie, see ya tomorrow mornin', but I still wan' out," blubbered the Mayor hanging up the phone, just wanting a couple more drinks.

He would finish the bottle and then go to bed or pass out on the floor, either way he knew he was going to tie one on, it was long overdue. He might make breakfast in the morning.

Immediately after hanging up with Dan, the chief made a call to the Judge, Bill to his close friends. Bill was at home enjoying one of his brothel videos from his library. He was not happy when he was disturbed.

"Hello," growled the judge.

"Bill, this is Reggie. We may have a potential problem," stated the chief.

"Oh, what's that?" asked Bill, obviously annoyed.

"Dan is drinking again. He called me and said he wanted out of 'The Club'. He's getting paranoid. He said they are all watching him and talking about him. I told him I'd talk to him in the morning at breakfast with June. What do you think?"

"Shit," exclaimed Bill. Reggie now had his full attention. He shut off the video and thought for a moment. "Talk with him tomorrow morning when he sobers up. See if he still maintains he wants out and let me know. We may have to have a jury session if he doesn't change his mind."

A jury session. That was not what the chief wanted to hear, although he had thought the same thing himself. There was not much else they could do if Dan still maintained he wanted out. You didn't just "get out" of 'The Club'.

"OK, I'll talk to you tomorrow morning after breakfast. I hope he comes to his senses by then," returned the chief hoping the Mayor's drunken paranoia wouldn't result in a jury session.

Jury sessions-that was where all the partners of 'The Club' held a meeting to determine the outcome of a disciplinary matter. They hadn't had a jury session in quite sometime.

The last session ended up in a strict warning to one of The Red Lantern's clients, Smokey, when he tried to find out the identity of Blaze. Luckily for Smokey, he heeded the warning, and no further action was needed, and he was kept as a client.

Nothing good could come out of a jury session, thought the chief. The Mayor could end up badly beaten or maybe even a contract placed on him, but that would be extreme. He would have to try to get Dan to forget about getting out of 'The Club', which would be the best outcome. The chief knew who the local partners of 'The Club' were, but not all, so he couldn't be sure of the result of any vote. The local partners were the judge, the Mayor, himself and June. He knew that any vote had to be unanimous for any serious penalties to be imposed. He also knew June was a close friend of the Mayor and she would try to protect him if it came down to a vote for any serious action to be taken.

The meetings were usually held by telephone conference, and only the judge knew who all the partners were. This was agreed to for security purposes, as large amounts of the money that were invested in the brothel and nightclub came from out of town and those partners didn't want their identities known to anyone. The mayor would not be invited to a jury session that was held about him; he would not even know about it, and the chief knew he couldn't say anything to him either.

***

Historic funds the city received from gaming taxes were a percentage of the gaming taxes paid to the state by the casinos. Historic funds were supposed to be used to fix-up and maintain historic structures in the city among other requirements. Much of the funds ended up being used for other priorities the city fathers designated. Many residents with structures needing repairs were not happy.

CHAPTER 19

Adam made the phone call to his FBI contact in Denver, Agent Brandon Kemp.

"Agent Kemp," Adam stated, "I spoke with the pastor and asked him to speak with the mayor and ask the necessary questions about the brothel and the poker games. He thought about it for a day, but wasn't comfortable with it and ended up declining. He didn't feel right being part of the investigation and wanted to end his participation in the whole matter."

"I thought he might," said Kemp.

"So I made an appointment with the mayor yesterday at noon, and asked the questions myself," Dan told the agent.

"How'd it go?"

He related to Kemp the mayor's responses and how nervous he seemed to have been, even to the point of going into a coughing fit. Adam then took particular pleasure at revealing to the agent his investigation into what the chief had told Brian.

"You're not going to believe this, but the chief called Brian and told him they had arrested two prostitutes in the casinos! I guess he thought that would end any suspicions Brian had."

"The chief must think everyone is as soft as he is."

"That's not all. I called a contact, a Deputy Sheriff friend at the Teller County Sheriff's Department, and asked him if any women were booked in last night for prostitution. He couldn't find anything, so I know the chief was making the whole story up in the hopes we would stop asking questions about the brothels and prostitution."

"Good work, Adam."

"There is another weak spot in what the chief did by falsely telling the pastor about the arrests," Adam continued to the Agent. "Every week the Police Department forwards to my newspaper, and all the other local papers, a list of all persons arrested the week before. Next week I'll check to see if they gave any names for the arrests or even if they include any arrests. The chief's secretary is the one who compiles the information and forwards it to the various newspapers, so the chief would have to either do it himself to continue the ruse, or somehow add the names into the compilation so the secretary can forward them."

"It's really hard to tell if the mayor knows the chief gave him false information, or if he is working with the chief to get us to back off asking questions about the prostitution bit," Adam stated.

Agent Kemp was impressed with the work Adam had accomplished.

"You should have been a cop instead of a reporter," exclaimed Agent Kemp, "You did a hell of a good job!"

"Well, any good reporter has to have a little hound dog in him," replied Adam grinning ear to ear, "I kind of enjoyed making Dan squirm a bit."

"I kind of caught that, Adam," stated Agent Kemp.

Adam was eager to obtain more direction and to harass the mayor some more. "Where do we go from here?" he asked.

"I can see you're having way too much fun with this, but we don't go anywhere right now. We wait. We stirred the pot a little; let's see what rises to the top. I'm willing to bet we'll see something happen, and soon."

"Alright, I'll stand down for now. Let me know if you need anything," stated Adam.

"I'll be in contact, let me know if you hear anything more," the FBI agent replied.

***

When gaming started, there was a great need to increase the size of the police department to accommodate the problems that came with thousands of daily visitors. There had always been a large turnover on the small police force, with young officers transferring to larger cities after they'd acquired some experience. The new graduates always wanted more action than a small town could provide, and the pay was usually better. The seasoned officers, many retired from larger cities, appreciated the relative tranquility of a small town, no matter what the pay.

CHAPTER 20

June seated herself at their usual table in the Terrace Restaurant of the Scarlet Rose Casino, waiting for the mayor join her for breakfast. She was early again and took the time to primp herself in the mirrored wall. She was surprised to see Chief Campbell's reflection approaching. She turned to greet him as he sat down next to her.

Terri, who always waited tables in the morning, knew June expected her regular carafe of iced tea and sugar packets, and brought them for her before the chief had a chance to speak. "Good Morning, June. Good Morning, Chief, it's a pleasure to see both of you this morning. What can I get for you to drink?"

"Coffee, black with sugar," he replied as though he was giving orders to one of his officers. Terri retreated to the kitchen to get the coffee.

"What brings you here this morning, Chief?" inquired June as she studied him.

The chief looked around the restaurant; they were the only customers except for an elderly couple seated two tables away.

He spoke in a low, serious voice, "We have a problem and I'm glad I caught you before Dan got here. He called me yesterday afternoon and he's been drinking again. He was really paranoid and said he was being watched and told me he wanted out of 'The Club'. I need you to help me talk to him this morning. He has to stop this paranoia. I'm afraid there will be a jury session if he continues to say he wants out."

June thought for a moment. "He's drinking again, huh? We can't have him go into rehab again. He needs to get a grip. I know every once in a while he's asked me if I've heard anyone talking about 'The Club'. He's never told me he wanted out though. I called Marcos and told him about it the last time. He said he would take care of it. I don't know if he did or not."

"I don't know where this will go, but if we don't rein him in..." the chief stopped. The mayor was walking through the entrance to the restaurant. "Here he is."

Dan was looking pretty ragged as he sat down at his regular seat across from June. The whites of Dan's eyes were as red as a Bloody Mary and his breath still reeked of scotch. His hair looked as though he passed a comb through it once and his clothes like he had slept in them all night. He was a mess.

"Did you wrestle with a Polar bear last night, Dan?" asked Terri with a smile as she brought the chief's and Dan's coffee to them.

Dan didn't answer.

"Anyone for breakfast?" she asked looking around the table.

The chief waved her off, "Not this morning." Terri left and went over to the elderly couple.

"Morning, Dan," said the chief, looking at Dan's eyes. "Tie one on last night?"

The chief was disgusted. Here was the political leader of the city and he looked like some bum off the street corner.

"My head hurts. I feel like a herd of buffalo ran through it," Dan replied, gulping down his coffee.

"Good, maybe you'll learn again that you can't drink. Remember? You're an alcoholic. What the hell are you doing?" The chief's voice was rising as he spoke. "Do you remember calling me yesterday?" He wanted to know if he remembered telling him he wanted out of 'The Club'.

"Yeah, I remember," replied Dan, "but just barely."

June had been quiet to this point. "What do you remember?" she asked, then added, "you look horrible, Dan."

Dan looked directly at the chief. "I told you I wanted out. I still do. Adam was asking me questions about the operation, and he didn't buy the story you told him. He didn't buy it when I told him either. He said it didn't seem to match the information he had. Then he asked about the poker games. I tell you, we need to shut the operation down or I want out."

"Is the alcohol finally rotting your brain?" questioned June, ticked off that Dan still was adamant about getting out. "What about your investment?" she asked.

"I'd like to get it back, sure," Dan stated slowly, "even if it's only a partial return. If I have to let it all go, so be it. I want out."

"A hundred thousand isn't a small sum, Dan, are you sure about this?" asked the chief, shocked that Dan was willing to give up that amount of money to get out of 'The Club'. He had inherited the money when his mother passed away and left him quite a large sum.

June knew she had to try to reason with Dan in his paranoid, delusional state of mind. She too was surprised he was willing to give up his invested money. He was her friend, though, and she didn't want to see him hurt. She knew there was a good chance of a jury session being called and didn't know how that would turn out. She made up her mind she was going to try to protect him if it came to that.

"Dan, why don't you think about this for a while before making a decision. Give it some time. This isn't something you should answer so quickly. But you have to stop your drinking. You know you can't handle it.

You're going to be like this everyday, all fucked up," June was getting serious, thinking of the possible consequences his actions could bring.

Reggie got up to leave. He took a last sip of his coffee and told Dan, "It's up to you. I'll give you until tomorrow morning to decide, and then I'll have to pass your decision on to the others. It'll be up to them how to handle it. Think about it and get back to me. I'll meet you here again for breakfast." The chief threw a couple bucks on the table to pay for his coffee and left.

June was the first to break the silence. "Dan, you can beat the alcohol again, I have faith in you. 'The Club' isn't going to take this lightly."

"I know, June, I doubt they will give me any of my investment back. But I doubt they will do anything else. Hell, I'm one of the founding partners in 'The Club', and I know too much. Besides, I'm pretty sure I've got your vote if it comes down to it," Dan stated with a wink.

"Be real careful, Dan, I don't know where this will take us. We're breaking new ground here with 'The Club'," said June, "I can only protect or help you so much."

"I appreciate anything you can do for me, June."

***

During the 1890s, many of the miners in the Cripple Creek area joined a miners' union, the Western Federation of Miners (WFM). A significant strike took place in 1894, marking one of the few times in history that a sitting governor called out the national guard to protect miners from anti-union violence by forces under the control of the mine owners. By 1903, the allegiance of the state government had shifted and Governor James Peabody sent the Colorado National Guard into Cripple Creek with the goal of destroying union power in the gold camps. The WFM strike of 1903 and the governor's response precipitated the Colorado Labor Wars, a struggle that took many lives.

CHAPTER 21

When Chief Campbell left the restaurant after talking with Dan and June, he went directly over to Judge William Tillis' house. The judge was expecting a full report from him.

Judge Tillis lived in the Cripple Creek Mountain Estates, about three miles northwest of the city. After his accident, he sold his two-story Victorian in the center of the city and had a wheelchair accessible home built in the 'Estates'.

The single story log ranch was impressive; vaulted polished oak beam ceilings gave the house an airy feel, its expansive and numerous windows brought nature in, along with considerable amounts of light. The floors were of smooth hardwood and tile, making it easy for Bill to maneuver his wheelchair from room to room. Two of the three bathrooms in the house were equipped to allow him easy access to the toilet. His personal bathroom had a roll-in shower stall, where he could switch from his wheelchair to a plastic chair to sit under the shower spray.

Reggie pulled around to the back of Bill's house and let himself in the back door.

The judge was waiting for him. "Well, what did he say?"

"He was pretty ragged Bill, hung over like a son-of-a-bitch. He still maintains he wants out though. I told him I would give him until tomorrow morning to give me a final answer. I left June to try to talk some sense into him. We'll see if she can."

"I'm going to have to notify the other partners we have a potential complication," stated the judge indicating the rest of 'The Club', "they'll be really pissed off if I withhold the information and it turns into a larger problem."

"I kind of thought you might have to," replied the chief, "But can't we wait until tomorrow morning when we'll know for sure? I know what's going to happen once we open that door."

Bill contemplated his options. He knew once he notified the other partners of 'The Club', they would push for a jury session. He didn't have any particular affinity for the Mayor, but he knew June was a close friend of Dan's, and, June was also a close friend of his. He didn't want to cause any unnecessary stress between him and June as it might interrupt his flow of C.D.'s, and she was his only source. Of course he couldn't say anything about that, no one else knew about them. The chief, he thought, could give a shit about Dan one way or the other.

"What if tomorrow morning Dan tells you he changed his mind and says he was temporarily fucked up, apologizes, and says he wants to continue in 'The Club'? He says all the right things. How long do you think it will be before he becomes paranoid again? How long do you think it's going to be before he starts drinking heavily again? If any cops from the county or state ever question him, do you think he would hold up, or collapse under the questioning? And what if the FBI ever comes back into town like they came after you; do you think he would hold up? There are several people who are depending on our judgment here, and they won't be polite if we choose the wrong options," the judge challenged. "I think we need to hold a jury session."

Reggie paced the floor for several minutes. "Make the calls," the chief told him, "I really don't trust the son-of-a-bitch right now. I don't see him quitting his drinking anytime soon and we certainly can't have him going into rehab again."

The chief listened as the judge made the calls to the three other partners of 'The Club' and briefed each of them on the status of Dan. They scheduled a conference call for eight that night. Now he had to call June and let her know, and that would be the toughest call of them all. This would be a jury session.

The judge dialed June's cell phone. She answered on the second ring.

"Hello, Bill, how are you?" June said.

"Call me back at home; by landline," the judge ordered and hung up.

***

June knew this didn't sound good, Bill had never ordered her to call his home phone by landline before. She rarely heard Bill sound like this, but wondered what it was about. Dan, maybe? She went to a pay phone and called the judge back at his home number.

"June," asked Bill, "Is Dan with you?"

"No," she responded, "He left about fifteen minutes ago."

"This isn't a social call. You know what is going on with Dan. We have a conference call tonight."

June was silent for several moments. She couldn't believe what she had just heard. _They were supposed to wait until tomorrow morning, she thought. They told him; they were going to give him until breakfast to change his mind. This wasn't fair at all._

"How can you do this to Dan, Bill?" June demanded. "Reggie gave him until tomorrow morning to change his mind. He still thinks he has until then."

The judge tried to make it as easy for June as he possibly could, but there was no easy way to tell someone that their friend is going before a jury session.

"Dan can't be trusted anymore. He started drinking again and you know we can't send him to rehab. Think about it, how long will it be before he wants out again? If anyone questions him, could he stand up to it? I don't think so, and not telling the other partners may be worse for us than having a jury session for Dan. It has to be this way, June," explained Bill.

June was pissed off now. "That may all be true," she stated, "but Reggie still gave him until tomorrow morning. If he comes around it may soften any punishment or fines 'The Club' votes on. Dan is not some Joe-shit-the-ragman off the street!" she yelled into the receiver, "He's one of us. This isn't fair!"

"I know, June, and you can bring all that up when we talk. Be available tonight at eight. Remember, landline only, no cell phones--or you can come over here," invited Bill. He didn't want any possibility of the jury session being intercepted.

June knew there was no debating the issue. He was the judge, and next to 'Marcos the Enforcer', he was the real 'Enforcer'. She would have to try and protect Dan as much as she could, and hoped there wouldn't be repercussions directed at her for doing so.

***

Through 2005, the Cripple Creek district produced about 23.5 million troy ounces (979 1/6 troy tons; 731 metric tons) of gold. The underground mines are mostly idle, except for a few small operations. There are significant underground deposits remaining, which may become feasible to mine in the future. Large scale open pit mining and cyanide heap leach extraction of near-surface ore material, left behind by the old time miners as low grade, has taken place since 1994 east of Cripple Creek, near its sister city of Victor, Colorado.

The current mining operation is conducted by Cripple Creek and Victor Gold Mining Company (CC&V). The mine operates 24 hours a day, 365 days a year. Mine operations, maintenance, and processing departments work a rotating day/night schedule in 12-hour shifts.

CHAPTER 22

As seven-thirty rolled around the chief arrived at the judge's house in his own vehicle. He didn't want to attract attention by driving one of the city's cruisers tonight. The chief stepped out of his vehicle and pulled out one of his expensive Cuban cigars. He inhaled the scent of it for a few seconds as he held it under his nose, finally clipping the tip, and lighting it.

The judge rolled his wheelchair out onto the wooden deck attached to the rear of his home.

"Got another one of those?" he asked. Only the chief had Cuban cigars and he rarely gave one up to anybody.

"I suppose I could spare one tonight," smirked the chief getting back into his car to retrieve another cigar. He climbed the three steps next to the handicap ramp, clipped the cigar and gave it to the judge.

"I have something to tell you," commented the judge puffing slowly on the cigar, "but it has to remain strictly between us. If it gets to June, we'll all probably be in the crapper."

"All right, what is it?" questioned the chief, taking a puff on his cigar.

"There's going to be two jury sessions tonight."

"What?"

"Hang on," continued the judge. "The first one is already set up. The verdict will be that Dan gets half his investment back but he must resign from the City Council at the next meeting. He can choose the reason he is resigning. In addition he must leave town within a month after the resignation. I need you to make that motion. It will be seconded by me and probably be a unanimous vote. I figure June will go for it also."

"Okay, I can do that."

The chief's eyebrows were scrunched together. He wondered what was coming next.

The judge continued, "After June leaves, there will be another jury session. We think June is too close to the mayor to make an impartial decision and the actual verdict needs to be decided by the remaining five of us. We can't take a chance on her saying anything to Dan that would screw things up."

"Agreed," stated the chief. He believed he had no options and had to go along with what the judge had set up. Besides, he believed the Judge was right.

They both enjoyed their cigars out on the deck with small talk for several minutes until June arrived. She pulled up to the rear of the judge's house, parked next to the chief's car and joined them on the deck.

"I feel like I should be smoking a cigar, too," she said smiling. "Or maybe I could just use a *big* cigar." She sighed dreamily.

The chief shot back. "Yeah, it must be tough to see a mile of cock come in the brothel every week and not be getting even an inch of it."

June laughed and rolled her eyes; Bill let out a belly laugh. He wasn't the only one not getting any from the brothel.

"I wouldn't want ninety-nine percent of that mile anyway," June shot back still laughing at the chief's remark. That brought even more laughter from the judge and chief, who were nodding in agreement.

"Let's go inside," said the judge as he turned electric wheelchair towards the door and placed his cigar in an ashtray that was sitting on the railing, "It's about time for the meeting." The chief placed his cigar in the same ashtray and followed them into the house.

The phone call was placed to the other three anonymous partners of 'The Club'.

June pleaded with the others to let Dan out of 'The Club' with minor penalties, which the others at first objected, then agreed with.

"I move that Dan gets half his investment back but he must resign from the City Council at the next meeting. He can choose the reason he is resigning. In addition he must leave town within a month after the resignation," the chief said.

"I second that motion," the judge stated.

It went just as the chief and judge had discussed. The conversations were short, mostly preconceived, and deliberated within the short span of time.

June voted with the others the way they expected her to in the affirmative. The three other partners followed suit.

"I don't want any part of Dan's penalties to be an unfortunate meeting with Marcos," stated June.

The chief looked at the judge. They both nodded.

"That won't be necessary unless Dan doesn't abide by what's decreed here tonight," the judge stated. "It'll be a clean break. I don't want any hard feelings that would give him reason to do anything stupid."

***

June was pleased with the outcome and she volunteered to inform Dan. Although she knew he wouldn't be pleased there had been a jury session without him, nor would he be very happy it was held before the next morning when he was given the option of retracting his decision, she knew he would be pleased he was finally let out of 'The Club' with such a minor slap on the hand; it would cost him fifty thousand dollars, half of his investment. Resigning his position as Mayor might be something he may have a problem with as it hadn't been discussed with him, June thought, but this wasn't going to be an option. He would have to resign.

The three briefly discussed when Dan should be notified of the decision.

"Okay," June stated, "it's decided then, I'll notify him in the morning at breakfast when we meet. In that way we'll know what his final decision is; not that it matters anyway. But now I have to get home with the kids."

"I'm going to stick around here with Bill for a little while and finish my cigar," Reggie stated.

June left feeling good that she had protected Dan.

***

As June left, both the chief and the judge were out on the deck relighting their thirty-dollar Cuban cigars. They started discussing what was going to happen in the next jury session with the other three anonymous partners of 'The Club'.

"When I last spoke with them, I think they were leaning towards a hit for this session," Bill told Reggie.

"I'm not surprised. Actually, when it comes down to it, I really don't give a fuck. He's always been a liability. He's a drunk and can't keep his mouth shut. Hell, the profits divided by six is better than divided by seven."

"I agree, of course," said the judge, "but this could be a problem with June, and we don't need that."

"I leave that to you."

Finished smoking their cigars, the two went inside. The judge placed the call and after identifications were made, a voice on the other end of the speaker announced, "I will be speaking for the three of us on this end."

The chief and judge acknowledged the announcement and went right to the point.

"How do you want to handle the situation?" the judge asked.

"The three of us agree there must be an elimination. He is too unstable to deal with and presents a real threat to our business interests and us. We cannot conceive of any other way to deal with the problem," came the reply. "We motion and second for elimination. You also have three votes 'for'. The ball is now in your court, we hope you will make it a unanimous decision"

The judge and chief looked at each other. There was already a majority vote for elimination, but Club rules called for a unanimous verdict in such instances where extreme penalties are called for. Their votes would make the difference between life and death.

"One moment," Bill said as he placed the phone on mute. "Well, now is the moment of decision," stated the Judge to the chief. "What's your vote going to be? Mine is the affirmative."

"I personally don't trust the son-of-a-bitch," stated the chief. "He's a huge liability and our livelihoods are at stake. I say *hell yes!*"

After releasing the mute button the judge stated, "We vote in the affirmative." The judge and chief had just issued their first death sentence.

"Good day, gentlemen." The judge hung up the phone and the two sat looking at each other. This was the harshest punishment meted out yet. There were no winners here, only a realization that there was no turning back.

The judge picked up his phone and dialed a number.

"Marcos, come see me. I have a job for you." There was a brief silence. "Good. See you then."

He looked at the chief. "He's coming to see me in the morning. I'll let you know."

"See you later. I'll be at home if you need me."

***

With many empty storefronts and picturesque, antiquated homes, Cripple Creek once drew interest as a semi-ghost town. At one point the population dropped to a few hundred, although Cripple Creek was never entirely deserted. In the 1970s and 1980s travelers on photo safari might find themselves in a beautiful decaying historic town. A few restaurants and bars catered to tourists who would pass weathered, empty homes with lace curtains hanging in broken windows.

CHAPTER 23

June went to the Terrace Restaurant to meet with Dan as planned. Nothing unusual in that; however, she was a bit nervous this particular morning, as she not only had to inform him of the jury session, but she also had to tell him he had to resign as mayor at the next Council meeting which was to be held in two days.

June knew as the others had stated, if he wasn't in 'The Club' he was of no use to 'The Club' as mayor. The plan was to get June appointed to the Council after the Mayor Pro-tem was sworn in as mayor. There, she could keep an eye on everything and be privy to the inner gossip of the city.

Dan showed up for breakfast on time, but June could tell he had been drinking again. He wasn't drunk, but his breath reeked of booze. The waitress brought their normal drinks. Conversation was nil. They both ordered breakfast from the menu and the waitress left. Dan was the first to break the silence.

"I still want out," Dan said looking around the restaurant without looking at June.

"It doesn't matter now," said June, "They already held a jury session. I mean, we held a jury session."

Now Dan looked at June intently. "I thought they were going to give me until this morning." he exclaimed in a low voice, "What are they doing?"

"I didn't know about it until after you left yesterday and I was ordered not to say anything to you. We had the session last night. I managed to help you somewhat, but not a whole hell of a lot. You're going to lose some money."

"I know it's not your fault. You said you would try to protect me, and I know you had to watch out for yourself also. I appreciate all you've done. So, what's the verdict?" asked Dan.

June smiled at Dan. "They ended up voting that you can get out, but you must give up half of your investment. That was a better outcome than I expected. I thought you would at least forfeit all your investment."

Dan was ecstatic. "June, I could give you a big kiss right here," he exclaimed. He was all smiles.

"Not so fast," stated June, more serious now. "There's more to it."

"What's that?" he asked, his smile leaving.

"You have to announce your resignation as Mayor. They will leave it up to you as to what reason you give, but that is part of the deal. I tried to convince them to let you stay, but there was no talking them out of that part."

She was lying to him, of course, about trying to talk 'The Club' out of it, but she also knew he would never know.

***

Dan was temporarily in shock. He hadn't planned on, or even thought they would demand anything like that. But what the hell, he thought, he was getting fifty thousand of his money back. That would make up for the resignation. His winning the mayor's seat was a fixed election to begin with anyway; his reward for having completed alcohol rehab.

"When do I get my money?" asked Dan, now thinking about where he was going to move, "and do I get part of this month's cut?" referring to the payouts from the brothel.

"The money will be coming in a few days. They said it would take a few days to get that much cash together.

As far as the cut, I wouldn't push it," replied June. "I'll see what I can do, but don't endanger the results of the session by pushing for too much."

"Okay, just asking," he replied.

"Let me give you a bit of advice, Dan," she said in a low voice. "Quit your drinking and get some help. Above all, never, ever, breathe a word about 'The Club' or anything associated with it. If you do, there will surely be another jury session, if you connect with what I mean," June said in her most serious voice. "I also protected you from a meeting with Marcos, but any screw-ups may void that agreement, or worse."

"I understand. Thanks."

They finished the rest of their breakfast making small talk, hugged each other, paid for their food, and left the restaurant. Both knew it would probably be their last breakfast together.

***

The gold-bearing area of the Cripple Creek district was the core of an ancient volcano within the central Colorado volcanic field, last active over 30 million years ago during the Oligocene age. Small amounts of free or native gold was found near the surface but at depth, plentiful un-oxidized gold tellurides and sulfides were found.

CHAPTER 24

Two days later the judge called Reggie and told him to come see him. The chief met him at his house.

"I've spoken to Marcos and the other partners of 'The Club'. The plan has been set in place for Dan. First, they want to wait for him to resign from his position. There will be less attention paid to him after a resignation than if he were still mayor. There will be some, but not much. He should resign on Wednesday at the next Council meeting."

"Next, we arrange to have Dan meet the person who is supposed to bring the money and pay him off. The plan is to meet him at the Garden of the Gods on Saturday, at the Three Graces, at five in the afternoon sharp, two days after Thanksgiving. The man will be dressed in a blue jacket and black hat and will have climbing gear with him; he'll be hard to miss. He'll tell Dan that a backpack with the money is waiting for him. From there, Dan will be taken to a secluded, popular climbing place in the Garden of the Gods where there will be a climbing accident."

"Marcos won't be there, will he? Dan will be immediately suspicious if he is."

"No, he won't be anywhere Dan can see him. The plan's simple, that's why I like it. Dan's a novice climber who was climbing at the Garden without a partner or the proper equipment. He was careless. He had been drinking. He also failed to get a permit as required. He had an accident, fell, and died from a head injury as a result of the fall."

The judge was to be notified when the plan was executed. Nothing could be traced to them; they weren't even involved except to pass on the information of where and when. If anything went wrong, they could claim complete innocence; plausible deniability.

The only hook in the plan was June. They would have to involve her in the payoff part of the plan, but she could not be advised of anything about the real plan.

"Let's let June give all the details to Dan. That way she would feel she was in the loop and not left out," stated the judge. "We'll tell her that Dan is to make the meet on Sunday. If we tell her Saturday, and he was found dead on Saturday or Sunday morning, she would suspect foul play."

They didn't want June to suspect anything but an accident. The judge would call Dan at the last minute on Saturday and tell him they had the cash and the day of the meeting had been changed. He was to immediately drive down to the Garden of the Gods in the Springs. To everyone else, it would look like he just went climbing, including June.

***

The Judge called June. "Would you like to call Dan and give the details of where he's to collect his money?

"Love to, Bill. I'm glad that the partners are allowing him an out like this."

***

June hit Dan's speed dial number. "Hi Dan. I have some information for you about "you know what." Let's meet."

"That's great. Where and when?"

"How about at The Miner's Pick, ten minutes."

"See you there."

***

When June gave him the details of the plan, he was ecstatic that the payoff was progressing so fast. He had worried that it may take months to get his money, even though he had been told it would be soon.

"I can't believe this whole thing is moving so fast. I thought it would be months before I'd see any cash. Now I can move on with my life. I think I'll rent my home out and take a long needed vacation. You know, I've got an old girlfriend I've been wanting to see out in Vegas, maybe play a little poker."

Vegas was looking real good to him right now.

***

On Wednesday night at Council meeting and with hat in hand, Dan made an announcement to the City Council, and those in attendance.

"I have made the decision to resign from my position of mayor, effective immediately. I have several health concerns that must be attended to, and I cannot fulfill my duties to the citizens of Cripple Creek at the same time. Thank you for your understanding and for the opportunity to serve this great city. The city will be in good hands under the leadership of the Mayor Pro Tem."

The Council and audience rose and gave Dan a standing ovation. He didn't take any questions and left it at that, allowing the rumors to ignite. He handed the gavel to the Mayor Pro Tem and left the meeting.

***

Saturday came fast for the chief and he was apprehensive until the plan was fulfilled. He nervously went about his business all day, including his routine Saturday fishing trip. He had to be home by three o'clock to call Dan to tell him the plans have changed and he was to be at the Garden of the Gods by five.

He thought about possible problems. Would Dan be home when he called? Would Dan be able to make it by five, as he would instruct him? Would he be sober? The chief couldn't control what Dan did or where he went on Saturday, he could only hope Dan would be available or that he could contact him by cell.

By noon, gray clouds loomed on the horizon. The wind was blowing and gusting with increasing intensity, and a light snow had started to fall. It wasn't sticking to the roads yet, but it was not looking good. The chief wondered if this could be one of those freak spring storms. He hoped not; he had watched the weather forecast the night before and although it was supposed to be cloudy and breezy, no snow was forecast for Cripple Creek or the Springs. The only predicted snow was supposed to stay to the north of the state, in the Aspen ski area.

By one thirty the chief packed up his fishing gear and headed home. It was colder now and the wind had not let up. The light snow had become heavier and had just started sticking to the roads. When he arrived home, he tuned to the weather report, which was now predicting three to five inches of snow for the mountain area in Teller County and the surrounding areas. Cripple Creek was in Teller County.

Now the chief was becoming worried. He called the judge.

"Hey, Reggie, everything okay?" greeted the judge.

"I'm going to call Dan earlier than planned," said the chief, "The weather report now says we're supposed to get three to five inches, so it may take him longer to get to the Springs."

"Really shouldn't be much of a problem, Reggie, he has four-wheel drive if he needs it. But, yeah, it may take a little longer to get there, so go ahead and make the call," instructed the judge.

After a few seconds, the judge changed his mind, "On second thought, go over to his house and tell him. Stay with him till he leaves. Make sure he doesn't call anyone about the change of plans, especially June."

They could not afford any screw-ups now. Everything had to go according to plan. The chief had no idea, however, how he was going to keep Dan from calling anyone if he wanted to. He would deal with it if it came up.

"10-4, I'll call you later."

The chief hung up and looked at his watch. It was two forty-four. He headed over to the ex-mayor's house.

When the chief arrived at Dan's house he observed his white Chevy Blazer in the driveway. He breathed a sigh of relief as he stepped upon the front porch and rang the doorbell. There was no answer. He felt his stomach start to turn. He rang the bell again this time holding the button down for several seconds. If Dan were asleep, this would wake him up.

***

Inside, at the first ring, Dan saw that Reggie was at the door. He quickly grabbed the mannequins that sat on his couch he had so many conversations with, and put them in the guest bedroom closet. He didn't want the chief to meet his relatives. As he placed the last one in the closet, the doorbell rang incessantly.

"I'm coming, I'm coming," yelled Dan.

He went to the front door and opened it. The chief had just turned to leave.

"I was in the bathroom," Dan said, "What's up?"

Reggie opened the screen door, stepped in, and looked around.

"Are we alone?" asked the chief.

"Yes, why?" replied Dan. "What brings you here?"

"There's been a change of plans. They want to get your money to you today. As a matter of fact, they're waiting in the Springs and will give you your money as soon as you can get there. They were worried this snow might intensify and not be able to make the transfer this whole weekend. I was kind of worried myself if you could even make it in this," said the chief trying to make it sound urgent that he leave now, "It's supposed to keep snowing."

"Don't worry, I can make it. I've got four-wheel drive if I need it. If they've got my money, I'm heading down there now," said Dan excitedly. "Any other change of plans, same place?"

"Everything else is the same. I'll call and tell them you're on the way. How long do you think the drive will take?"

"An hour and a quarter at the most, unless there's an accident or something that'll hold me up in traffic."

"Are you sure you want to go today in this snow, Dan? It looks like this storm is intensifying."

"If they've got my money, I'm going. I don't want to disappoint them," Dan intoned with sarcasm.

"All right, call me if there are any problems," the chief told him.

Dan grabbed his coat and was ready to head out the door. The chief was right in front of him. Everything was progressing as planned. The chief went to his vehicle and waited as Dan started up his Blazer and cleaned the snow off the windows. He watched him head out of town and up Tenderfoot Hill.

The chief would now wait for the call.

CHAPTER 25

Six o'clock came and went as the judge sat next to his phone at his home. He hadn't yet received the call he was waiting for. As soon as Dan was assassinated, the judge was to be called and assured that everything had gone as planned. The snow continued to fall, and there was now about four inches on the ground. The roads were not as bad, with only a couple inches in depth, but they were slick. The chief would also be waiting for a call from the judge, for the same reasons; both on pins and needles waiting for the call.

At six-twenty, the phone rang and the judge received an ominous call from Marcos.

"Where's the mayor?" he questioned. "My people said he never showed. They just left the Garden a few minutes ago."

"What?" asked the judge. "He left here around ten after three. He should have been there around quarter after four." After a slight pause he continued, "We'll have to check with the Sheriff's department and the State Police and see if there were any major accidents; maybe he was held up. He should have been there a long time ago. I'll get back to you."

Bill was puzzled. The chief had called him when the Mayor left and the chief had watched him until he was on Highway 67 heading up Tenderfoot Hill towards Colorado Springs. The chief also told him that Dan seemed really eager to collect his money. If he didn't get to the Springs, where did he go or what happened to him? Was there an accident that delayed him? The judge knew the chief was best suited to find out the answer to these questions, he had the contacts. He called him.

"Hello, Bill. I assume the job is complete," the chief said answering the phone.

"Hell, no," exclaimed the judge, "get your butt over here. We have a problem."

"Be right there," the chief replied.

Reggie arrived at Bill's house in ten minutes, parked in the back of the house, and climbed the rear steps to the back door. He knocked once and let himself in.

"Come on in," said the Judge as he poured himself a scotch on the rocks, "I can't figure out what we're up against or what's going on here. I thought we had everything running smoothly, all the details planned almost right down to the minute."

"We did," replied the chief chewing on the butt end of a cigar, "Everything went as planned. What's the problem?"

"He never showed up. Marco said his people left the Garden a few minutes ago. I just received a call from him wondering where Dan was. You need to start making calls to see if you can find him. With this snow, I don't know, maybe he had an accident or maybe he was held up by an accident."

"I told him to call me if he had any problems. He was real anxious to get his money, so if he went to the wrong place I think he would have called me by now. I'll call the Sheriff's Department, see if there were any accidents. Are you sure they didn't miss him?'"

"Did you get a call from him saying, 'Where are they?'"

"No."

"Then I guess he didn't show up. These guys are professionals, not some gang-bangers wanting a couple of quick bucks. Did you happen to call his cell phone?" The judge was grasping for any leads.

"He doesn't have one. He turned his cell into the city when he resigned from office and he hadn't picked up a new one yet. I'll call you if I find out anything."

***

Reggie headed to his office to make the official call to the Sheriff's Department. There were no accidents reported involving a white Chevy Blazer. The Chief called the hospitals in Colorado Springs. No unknown admissions and no admissions with a name of Daniel Comeau.

Now he was even more puzzled. The Sheriff Department's jurisdiction would only take Dan down a little past Woodland Park and Green Mountain Falls. After that, the El Paso County Sheriff's office would have jurisdiction, and then, the Colorado Springs Police Department.

He called the El Paso Sheriff's Department and the Colorado Springs Police Department with the same results; no Dan, no white Chevy Blazer, and no unknown persons injured.

It was now a little after seven and the chief wanted to call June to find out if she knew anything. If she did, he thought, how would he explain the change of plans? He had to take the chance; besides, he'd let the judge give details to her. She was probably going to find out sooner or later anyway.

June was just heading down to the Red Lantern for her job as madam when the chief called.

"Hi, Chief. What's up?" asked June.

"June, I need to see you. Can you come over to my office?"

"Now? I was just heading down to my other job."

"Please. It's important."

June knew it must be important, the chief *never* says 'please'.

"Be there in a few minutes."

It was still snowing hard and the snow was piling up fast. The wind had picked up, it looked like a full scale blizzard. At times it was a complete whiteout. Fifteen minutes later June arrived at the Police Station; she was completely covered in snow, was let in by the dispatchers and went upstairs to the chief's office.

"June, have you heard from Dan tonight?" he questioned still chewing on the cigar.

"I had a voicemail left on my phone a couple hours ago. Dan said some plans had changed and he was going to pick up some lettuce. I assumed he was picking up his money. I was going to call you tomorrow and ask why the plans changed," she told the chief, "Why? What's the problem?"

"Dan never made the contact with the people delivering the money. He was supposed to be there about four. They waited for him till about six and then Bill got a call inquiring as to his whereabouts, and Bill called me. Dan looked enthusiastic to get his money this early, but now he seems to have disappeared off the face of the earth. I called all the departments from here to the Springs and checked all the hospitals. Nothing."

"Did you check his house to see if he ever left?"

"He left all right. I was with him at his house and watched him as he headed up Tenderfoot Hill. He seemed anxious to collect his cash. The only thing I can think of is he ran off the road somewhere between here and Divide. I guess I'll have to go out in this snow and see if I can find any tracks."

"I doubt you'll be able to see anything, Reggie, it's a complete white-out and it's coming down so fast any tracks that may have been left will be gone by now. You better wait until tomorrow or when this storm breaks."

***

The chief knew she was right, and he didn't really want to go out looking for the mayor anyway, but others would probably want him to. They had to know where he was. He was a loose cannon and knew too much.

"I'll notify the Sheriff's Department to be on the lookout, and I'll take a quick ride. If I can't see anything, I'll come back and wait until tomorrow," decided the chief.

"You might want to call the State public works guys who are out there plowing. They would probably see something before the Sheriff's Department would," suggested June.

"Good idea," he replied.

The chief made the call to the public works department and was told the snowstorm was the most intense between Divide and Cripple Creek, eighteen miles of winding mountain road. They had two plow trucks continuously plowing between the two towns and were barely keeping up with the rate of snow, but they hadn't seen any accidents so far and that the roads were very slick.

The chief headed for his car to go look for Dan himself. When he stepped outside and saw the depth of the snow and the rate it was falling, he realized it would be futile. He turned around and went back inside to call Bill.

He placed the call and gave the judge the news he'd garnered from the various police agencies and hospitals he had contacted.

"We have got to find him," the judge made clear, "We can't leave loose ends like this."

"I know," replied the chief, "But I can't do anything until tomorrow. This storm is supposed to break sometime tonight. I'll start a search first thing tomorrow."

***

At daybreak, the chief went to the station early. Before leaving to look for the mayor, he again called all the local law enforcement agencies and hospitals he had contacted the night before, but to no avail. This time he made all the agencies aware that the ex-mayor of Cripple Creek has been missing since the storm and gave instructions to call the police department if he was located.

The chief grabbed the keys to his cruiser and headed out to canvass the road and ravines between Cripple Creek and Divide. The roads were partially cleared and were still very slick with a thin coat of packed snow. The snow had stopped around four in the morning and had accumulated a total of about ten inches. The sun shone brightly as it usually did after a mountain storm, and the early morning glare made driving even more hazardous.

He slowly traveled the eighteen miles to Divide looking for any sign of an accident or vehicle going off the road. He stopped in several places to look over the edge of the road where there were no guardrails down into the deep ravines. He could find nothing and returned to his office. His stomach was getting an uneasy feeling. Had Dan been playing him all along, acting like he was anxious to get his money? Did he discover what the real payoff was going to be? Did he become so paranoid that he went to a law enforcement agency and spilled his guts for some kind of deal?

These questions ate at him as he sat at his desk drinking his coffee. He had to call the judge soon and give him the bad news. Bill would have to call the rest of the partners. Would they have to shut down their business? Has everything been compromised? There was nothing they could tell until Dan surfaced somewhere, anywhere.

The chief called the judge and let him know what the results of the search had been. The judge was calm but noticeably upset.

"Shut the Red Lantern operations down until further notice. We have to know where he is, where he went," the judge instructed.

"That's going to piss off a lot of customers, Bill, do you think that's wise?"

"I don't care who gets pissed off, it's our asses if he is talking to the state guys or Feds or whoever. We have to know."

That night at around ten-thirty, the chief went to Dan's house to look for anything that may incriminate him or reference 'The Club'. The doors were locked and the windows latched. He knew he would have to figure out a way to get in. He didn't want anyone to see him in the house, but if someone did, there should need a good legal reason to be there. He left the house and returned to the police station. He would need help to fulfill his plan.

CHAPTER 26

China Doll was in a quandary; she had been notified the brothel was shut down and she was to have a visit from the Colonel tonight. She was told he would be delivering extremely important documents and she was to transfer them to the consulate the very next morning.

She arrived at eight that night in order to make sure she had a good location on the street to spot the Colonel. She didn't think he would be there until later, probably around eleven, but couldn't be sure. Tao decided to wait across the street from the nightclub where she could see the entrance to the nightclub, and catch him when he arrived.

In a way she was relieved the brothel was closed-- she wouldn't be subjected to his sexual whims. She laughed silently as she remembered the last encounter and his <u>huge</u> dong.

He could arrive anytime. She passed the time watching every passer-by, studying, and listening to music. She fretted about missing him and wondered what the consequences would be. She really didn't want to know.

Eleven rolled around slowly. The nightclub was hopping with many customers coming and going and China Doll recognized several of her clients. She was worried she may have missed the Colonel while studying.

Eleven-thirty. Where was he? Could she have really missed him? Her stomach sank as she looked at her watch and realized he had never been this late before. She thought about making a call to her contact at the consulate, but that would take her away from her lookout, and she didn't dare use her cell phone. No, she had to wait.

Eleven thirty-five. There he was, walking casually into the Thunderhead nightclub. She ran across the street, into the nightclub and tapped the Colonel on the shoulder. "Come outside," she stated. He followed her out the door. Outside, she told him, "The Lantern is temporarily closed. Follow me in your car."

Tao ran back to her vehicle and slowly headed over to a parking lot located next to the bank. She made sure the Colonel was following her. The parking lot was dimly lit, no one was around, and there was no traffic. She considered it a good place to exchange the documents the Colonel was supposed to bring. He pulled behind Tao's vehicle, got out of his car, quickly scanned the area, and got into hers.

"The Lantern has been closed for repairs for a few days, there was a water leak that flooded some rooms. I didn't know of any other way to inform you," she told him.

"That's bullshit, it sounds like they could have opened some of the rooms at least. This isn't secure. I don't like being out in the open."

Tao wasn't in the mood to put up with his crap after waiting so long.

"Well I don't like it either, I've been waiting here for you since eight o'clock, so that's the way it is. Do you have the documents?"

The Colonel pulled the documents from under his shirt and gave them to Tao. "Tell them I'll have the rest real soon." He opened the door and went back to his car. Tao sped off. She didn't want to give him a chance to come back and demand any services.

As the Colonel started to drive off, he scanned the area for anyone lurking in the shadows. His heart skipped a beat and then raced as he noticed a camera at the bank pointing his way. This was a substantial breach of security and would have to be rectified.

CHAPTER 27

It took about two hours for FBI Special Agent Spencer White to make the drive from Denver to Cripple Creek. The Agent on Duty received a call about the homicide at the Bank of Cripple Creek at 9:14 a.m. and Spencer was on his way within minutes.

Although he had not received any information that the homicide involved any stolen money from the bank, he had to make an appearance, gather information and any evidence in case he needed to take over the investigation. Very few bank robberies involve any homicides, but he couldn't be sure with the limited information he had.

Before White left, the FBI Agent in Charge of the Denver area called Spencer into his office and briefed him on an on-going investigation in Cripple Creek. An undercover FBI agent was already working in Cripple Creek. He was not told who the undercover agent was or why he was there, that was on a need-to-know basis; only that there was one and that he probably wouldn't run into him. He was also told by the Agent-in-Charge he doubted the homicide had anything to do with the undercover operation. White figured the undercover agent was probably involved in some high-level operation as he was told any further information would be given on a need-to-know basis only, and right now he didn't have a need-to-know.

Agent White arrived at the bank at approximately 11:35 a.m. after the two-hour drive from Denver. He flashed his badge and identification to the police officer guarding the front door and entered the bank. There he found a multitude of departments already taking statements, collecting evidence and investigating the murder.

"Who's in charge here?" asked White to no one in particular. Everyone looked over to see who was asking, and then went back to his or her prior conversations and work.

"Can I help you?" inquired Chief Campbell looking up at the six foot-two agent.

"I'm Special Agent Spencer White, FBI," he stated showing the chief his identification, "What do you have?"

Campbell was unimpressed, but polite. Since they weren't here to investigate him, he figured he might as well be as cooperative as possible.

"So far we only have a homicide," replied the chief, "We were waiting for you before we allowed the bank manager back in to check whether anything is missing."

Agent White was lead to the manager's office to view the body and the crime scene. He walked into the office and noticed that the deceased woman had a gold necklace, gold tennis bracelet and two diamond rings still in place. He thought to himself it would be unusual for those items to be left if this was indeed a robbery, unless whoever did it was in a tremendous hurry.

"OK, if that's all we have, then I'm heading back to Denver after the manager does the check," stated White. He observed one of CBI's agents he had worked with in the past writing in the corner of the bank. "I see the CBI is here. They can take over the investigation if that is all we have. They can forward all the information to me later."

***

Campbell was glad to hear it. He didn't need the FBI in his town any longer than necessary and hoped

White would head back to Denver as quickly as he had arrived. As far as he was concerned, The FBI was just a pain in his ass and wasn't going to do diddly-squat to help solve the murder.

***

The bank manager, Sandra, was called on her cell and asked to come back to the bank. This time, Agent White would need her to do a complete check of the bank and a count of the cash to see if anything was missing.

Spencer figured it would take awhile for her to come back and check everything out. The CBI was busy pulling fingerprints off everything, photographing and processing the crime scene. He thought he might as well get a cup of coffee and maybe a bite to eat while he waited for the bank manager to arrive.

"Chief, is there anywhere to get a cup of coffee around here besides the casinos?" asked Spencer.

Reggie briefly considered inviting the FBI agent to the police station where they always had a pot of coffee on, but his innate hatred of the Feds got the best of him. "Go up to Bennett and take a right. Down the street a few blocks, there's a place called Ralf's Breakroom on your left. They always have pretty good coffee. Tell Roxie I sent you and she'll take care of you."

***

The chief could have kicked himself for saying that, he didn't really want anyone to take care of a Fed. As a matter of fact, he just wanted him out of his city as soon as possible.

"Hell, I'll even buy you a cup of coffee if it'll get you out of my town faster," the chief thought.

***

Spencer got back into his black Ford Crown Victoria and drove down to Ralf's where he found a parking space on Bennett Avenue, across the street from the restaurant.

Spencer crossed the street and entered the cool building. He was surprised by the size of the business; a family-type restaurant greeted him just inside the entrance. Further back through an archway there was a bar area and beyond that pool tables and a small stage.

As his eyes adjusted to the dim light, a white board to the right of the archway indicated that he should check in with the bartender before taking a seat in the restaurant. He sat down at the bar. As he quickly looked the place over he saw a large round wooden beam above him spanning the bar from one end to the other. On it, he observed notches cut into the wood. Some appeared to be fresh; others older. If some of the marks hadn't been fresh, he would have assumed the log had been that way for a long time. Odd. What did they mean? For some reason, the notches intrigued him.

Instead of meeting Roxie, tending bar was Ted, a 20's something, handsome, muscular man with a full head of dark brown hair and a deep tan. He wore his black Ralf's t-shirt with the sleeves cut off, baring his powerful arms. He looked like he was a serious weightlifter, and sported a small diamond stud earring in his left ear.

***

Roxie was the bar manager and had hired Ted several months back. She really liked his demeanor with the customers, and besides, to her, he was kind of sexy. He treated all the locals really well, but didn't put up with any bullshit. Anyone trying to start a fight would be immediately escorted to the door. Those that didn't want to leave were helped out the door one way or another. He wasn't afraid to take anyone on and those who tried were soon to learn the hard way. When Roxie asked him where he'd learned all that, he'd just say he was 'taught'. She left it at that.

"What'll ya have?" Ted asked as he wiped down the bar. He was surprised to see a "suit" in Cripple Creek, especially in Ralf's.

"Just a coffee," replied Spencer, "touch of cream and two sugars."

"What's with the notch marks in the beam?" he inquired of Ted pointing at the beam above him. The marks reminded him of the old westerns with gunslingers putting notch marks on their guns for each person they delivered to God.

"Don't know," Ted replied shrugging his shoulders. "I think they've been there for awhile. I asked Roxie, the manager here, about them once and she just smiled and said no one seems to know. I haven't been here long enough to press it, maybe someday I will if I catch someone cutting any of the notches."

Ted gave him a smile and poured the coffee, brought over a mini pitcher of creamer, and a canister of sugar. He wasn't going to mess up anyone's coffee by adding them himself. Too many customers were finicky about their coffee.

"So, what are you selling?" asked Ted, trying to make a little conversation. He was positive the customer was a salesman, probably pushing office supplies, restaurant supplies or insurance, he thought.

"Nothing," retorted Spencer rolling his eyes. He wasn't really in the mood for any more small talk.

"Oh?" questioned Ted who now had his interest piqued. "It's rare we see suits around unless they're salesmen or a lawyer. As a matter of fact, I haven't even seen anyone in a suit around here for over a week."

"I'm with the FBI," stated Spencer, "there was an incident at the bank this morning. I'm here on that. I just needed a cup of coffee then I have to go back."

"An incident?" exclaimed Ted smiling broadly, "must be more than 'an incident' for the FBI to be here."

Spencer didn't want to say anything else. He didn't want conversation right now. He was thinking of the homicide and how strange it seemed to be.

"You'll have to read about it in the newspaper," Spencer told the nosey bartender, "make this coffee to go, please."

He left Ralf's and headed back to the bank. When he arrived, he noted a car pulling into the parking lot. A woman stepped out and headed toward the bank. At the front door Spencer stopped and turned toward Sandra, "Are you the bank manager?" he inquired.

"Yes, I am. Sandra O'Brien," she replied putting out her hand, "And you?"

"Spencer White, FBI", he replied, shaking her hand, "I hope everything is in order. How long for you to check?"

"Only a few minutes," she stated, "I just need to look at the drawers and the night deposits. The vault wasn't opened and the ATM is still secure."

"Great," Spencer said, "I've got a lot of work waiting for me back at the office. If this is just a homicide, CBI will have jurisdiction and I need to get back to Denver." He really hoped that was all it was.

***

Just a homicide! Sandra thought to herself. *What a piece of work he is. Norma was a flesh and blood person, a friend; someone loved by the whole city. How could he callously dismiss her as 'just a homicide?'*

Spencer followed her into the bank and sought out the chief.

"Anything new?" he inquired.

"Not really," the chief replied, "the place was clean, no casings, no gun; we don't even have a suspect. There are so many fingerprints, of course that won't help right now. Oh, and we found one bullet in the wall, but it is pretty deformed. Norma has two entry wounds in the head, so she probably still has one."

"We'll look for it at the autopsy." Spencer looked around, he was anxious to leave. "It says on the front door the bank only has drive-thru on Saturday mornings. Is that true?" questioned Spencer.

"Yes, and the responding officers reported to me the front door was unlocked allowing them to make an entry without incident."

The chief hated even talking to the Fed.

Sandra chimed in as she listened to the chief, "That's unusual. I know Norma wouldn't have left the door unlocked, she was very particular about things like that."

"Mr. White," Sandra called out, "The night deposits are missing and all of the cashier's drawers are still locked. What do you want me to do?" she inquired.

"See if you can get me a list of the missing night deposits and a count of the cash if you can." The Chief thought Spencer sounded different now. He sounded in charge. "I also need to know what check deposits were taken and those exact amounts."

Sandra knew this was going to take awhile. She was going to have to find out who regularly made night deposits on Friday nights or early Saturday mornings, find out if they made one last night, and how much. Just the phone calls would take most of the day she figured. This wouldn't be easy with Norma's body lying just feet away. She didn't know how long she could maintain her composure and just do the work. It had to be done, but that didn't make it any easier.

***

Spencer walked over to Reggie. "Chief, we also have a robbery, so, I'm taking over the investigation. I need everyone to leave now and I'll call in my team to process the bank," Spencer stated matter-of-factly. "Would you please let the other departments know? I have to call Denver. Everyone goes except the bank manager. I need the names and departments of every person who has been on scene. Could you get that for me?"

The chief was steaming. Now he would have to put up with the Feds probably for days, and they were already starting to use him as an errand boy. Plus he was now going to call for a whole damn team of Feds. This was his town, wasn't it?

"Yeah, sure, I'll take care of that."

"Oh, and would you do a notification of next of kin?"

Spencer was really pushing the chief's buttons now.

"Do you know if she was married? If she was I need her husband's information so we can contact him later."

Why don't the Feds do their own work the chief thought? *How come inter-agency cooperation always consists of us doing the cooperation and the legwork?*

***

Spencer's mind was now clicking at high-speed. He was going thru what he knew about the crime scene; what to report to his bosses in Denver, making mental and physical notes.

There were two shots to the right temple, probably a thirty-eight or nine millimeter from what he could see, an open front door, night deposits missing, no weapon, and no bullet casings which indicated to him either a revolver or a professional hit; and Norma's jewelry was still intact. Whoever killed her was probably waiting for her and followed her in when she unlocked the front door. He went back to Sandra.

"Where is the recorder located?"

Sandra looked up from the counter. "It's in the office...where Norma is at."

She wouldn't to go to the room to show him. She didn't want to see the gruesome scene. "It's in the cabinet to the right as you enter the room."

Spencer went into the office and opened the wooden cabinet in the corner of the room. He found the recorder and pushed the eject button. Nothing happened. He looked in the recorder. The CD was gone.

CHAPTER 28

Spencer looked over the body as he waited for the Coroner to arrive. He could see only one exit wound on Norma's head. He would have to wait for an autopsy for confirmation, but he could find only one bullet hole in the wall.

"Thirty-eight caliber?" he guessed out loud. "Low velocity?"

Agent White called Denver, reported his findings to the Agent in Charge and asked for a forensics team. He was told they would be on their way and would be there about three. Spencer went back to Sandra.

"The CD is missing, it must have been taken by the assailant. Norma must have told him where it was before she was shot."

Sandra gasped holding her hand to her mouth, "Oh, shit! I forgot all about it."

"Forgot about what?" he asked

"We just installed another recording system last week. We are supposed to use both of them for a couple of months before we take out the old CD system. We had to be sure the new one was working well, and see if there were any problems. The new system is a digital recorder. I can download the recording to a disk for you. I doubt Norma would have told anyone about that one."

Spencer was ecstatic. "Where is it?" he asked.

"It's in the closet, over there," she said pointing to a door across the room.

Spencer went over to the closet. It was locked.

"Do you have the key?" he asked.

"Yes," Sandra said hesitantly, "It's in my desk, top right hand drawer. Can you get it? I really don't want to go in there. It has a white tag on it that says 'Digital Recorder'."

Spencer notated in his notebook what he was doing in the crime scene, specifically removing the key from the top right drawer of the desk. It didn't affect the placement of the body, so he opened the drawer, found the key, and removed it shutting the drawer to its original position.

"This is great," stated Spencer walking over to the closet, "This will really help. I hope it's been recording, it'll tell us a lot."

Sandra came in the room and walked over to the closet with the agent, averting her eyes away from Norma. Spencer unlocked the door and opened it. The recording light was on.

"It looks normal, do you want me to download for you?" asked Sandra.

"No, please don't touch a thing," replied Spencer, "My people will take care of it. I don't want to chance anything going wrong. We need that recording."

"Alright, it's all yours."

"How long has this system been recording?"

"About three weeks now. I don't think there has been any downloads since it was installed. I know no one has been here to service it since it was started. All I was supposed to do was check the recording light each day and call in if it wasn't on."

"How often are you supposed to download or change disks?"

"We haven't been told to do anything yet, but I understood that it will record about a month without overwriting."

Spencer recorded all the information in his notebook and thanked Sandra.

"For Norma's sake, I hope it was operating normally," stated Sandra.

"Me too," Spencer said.

CHAPTER 29

June was having breakfast alone at the Scarlet Rose when a large figure loomed over her. Uninvited, he sat down with her. Dismissing the normal pleasantries, the chief started right in grilling June.

"Are you sure you haven't heard from Dan? It's been almost a week and no one has seen or heard from him."

"I really resent your tone *and* your line of questioning, Reggie."

June glared at him. Through clenched teeth, she continued, "Whatever you may think about my friendship with Dan, we aren't really that close. I've never been to his place, or he to mine. I have told you repeatedly that I have not heard from him. If I had, I would have told you and the judge. I know what side my bread is buttered on. I'm worried about him, but not in the way you appear to be. As paranoid as he seemed to be, I really don't think he'd give any of us up."

Reggie felt the blood rushing to his face. He was getting nowhere with June. She seemed pretty steadfast about not having heard from Dan. He reflexively pounded his fist down on the table, sending dishes and June jumping.

He took a deep breath. "Sorry, June. This is just so frustrating. Where in the hell did he go?" Exasperated, Reggie let out a deep sigh, leaned back in his chair and examined the ceiling.

Dan had no family they knew of. He was an only child, had never married, and was a confirmed bachelor. Both of his parents were deceased. They had no idea whom to contact if they found him dead somewhere, but right now the chief was thinking about protecting himself and 'The Club', but mainly himself.

"We have to get in his house and look for anything he might have there that may affect us. If he kept any records or journals, we need to find out and get rid of them. I hope he was careful enough not to keep any large sums of cash lying around."

"I agree, but how are we going to get in?" asked June.

"Leave that to me, I'll take care of it. We need to get a news release out that he's missing so everyone can be on the lookout for him. I'll have to give the newspaper some bullshit story of how he was going to the Springs to go climbing and hasn't been seen since. That's all they need to know for now."

"You know the reporters are going to ask questions, Reggie, especially since he went down to the Springs in a snow storm and you were the last person to see him alive. And if you open the door with a news conference or a release, there's going to be questions about his sudden resignation as mayor too. You need to be ready with plausible, airtight answers."

"I said I'd handle it. But I need you to make a call for me tomorrow," Reggie directed. "At around ten tomorrow morning, I want you to make a call to the police station. Identify yourself and tell the dispatcher you would like for the police to check on the ex-Mayor. Tell them you usually have breakfast with him every morning and he hasn't shown up the past week and he doesn't answer his phone. You are afraid something has happened to him as he doesn't answer his door either."

"What's that going to do?"

"It gives us a legal reason to break into his house to check on him. It's called a 'health and welfare' check. Sometimes people who live alone, die or have strokes or heart attacks in their homes and no one knows about it for days or weeks. Many times we have a concerned friend or relative who will call us to check on them, and with no other alternative, we break in; gain access that is, and check on the person. Usually we have the fire department do the entry for us. That is what I intend to do."

"All right, I'll take care of that part. Ten o'clock."

***

At ten the next morning the chief made sure he just happened to be in the dispatchers office looking at reports. At ten after ten the call came in from June. The dispatcher assured her they would look in on the ex-mayor.

"I'll take care of that. Call Officer Sanborn on the radio and tell him to meet me at Dan's house," he instructed the dispatcher.

When the chief arrived at Dan's house, Sanborn had already arrived.

"Sarge, we need to do a welfare check on Dan. No one's seen or heard from him for almost a week. We're all pretty concerned."

The Sergeant checked the doors and all the windows and reported them secure. He knocked on the door and rang the doorbell for several minutes with no results.

"Call the fire department and ask for assistance," ordered the chief, "the Officer on Duty will probably ask what is needed. Just tell him the Police Chief wants assistance for a 'health and welfare' entry."

Fifteen minutes later a rescue truck from the fire department pulled up behind the chief's cruiser in front of Dan's house.

"Sergeant, You can clear now. I'll take care of it from here."

"10-4, Chief."

The Lieutenant in charge found the chief. "What do you have, Chief?"

"The former mayor has been missing for about a week and friends are concerned he may have hurt himself or might have a medical condition. We need to get in and check on him. There's been no response from inside."

"Okay, let me take a look and see where the easiest entry point is." The Lieutenant walked around the house checking all the windows and doors, searching for a way in.

"I think we'll just break a small pane of glass in the rear door, chief. Looks like that will be the least amount of damage and the easiest to fix."

"Sounds goods," the chief agreed.

The Lieutenant had one of his men break one the small panes of glass in the wooden framed door. He reached in, unlocked and opened the rear door to the house.

"There you are, Chief," the Lieutenant stated.

The chief and Lieutenant entered the house and checked each room and the basement. There was no sign of Dan.

"I'll take care of securing the house," the chief told the Lieutenant. "I'll call a carpenter from the city to board up the window."

"All right, we'll clear," the Lieutenant responded as he exited the house. "Have a good day."

Everything was going as the chief had planned. Now he had the freedom to look for any incriminating evidence of 'The Club'. He walked the rooms, searching for anything obvious. In the corner of one of the bedrooms a computer was sitting on an antique maple desk. He turned it on and scanned the directory. A folder marked "CLUB" stood out and Reggie clicked on it. The computer asked for a password.

"Shit," he yelled. "What would he use for a password?" he thought to himself. He tried several words he thought Dan might use, to no avail. He saw that whatever was in the file was small. The chief found a disk, copied the file, put it in his pocket and turned the computer off. He would study it at home.

In the master bedroom, he searched everywhere. In the closet he observed the sports coat Dan seemed to wear daily and checked the pockets. Inside the left breast pocket he found a small daily calendar notebook. Figures written in on each Friday stuck out at the chief. These were records of money paid to him each week as his cut from 'The Club'. He thumbed through the rest of the book. On the last page in very small print was the word "THOMASPERRY". "What the hell was that?" he wondered aloud. That was June's son's name. *Could that be the password?* He put the book in his pocket with the disk.

It had been almost an hour since the fire department left and he still had to call a carpenter to fix the window. Reggie called the police station.

"Call the public works department and have someone come over and patch the door. Tell them the fire department had to break a window to gain access to Dan's house."

Now he'd only have a short time until someone arrived.

The chief used the remaining time to search through the desk the computer sat on. In the bottom drawer he found labeled file folders containing important and semi-important documents. One of the folders was labeled 'WILL'. He pulled out the folder. Inside he found an envelope that read 'LAST WILL AND TESTAMENT of DANIEL COMEAU'. He placed the envelope in his coat pocket. *Depending on what's in it, it might see the light of day,* he thought.

He turned the computer back on wanting to see if he had discovered the password in the notebook. He clicked on the 'CLUB' file, and entered the word 'THOMASPERRY'. He was in! The file contained all of the payments Dan had ever received from 'The Club'; there were hundreds of thousands of dollars notated. He had a copy of the file in his pocket, so he erased the file from the computer. Now, where was the money? He knew Dan couldn't put it in the bank. None of the members could.

A knock at the door halted the chief's sleuthing. It was Jessie, an employee from the public works department. Reggie let him in and directed him to the rear door that needed to be secured. Jessie assessed the damage and said he would be right back with the necessary equipment and supplies to temporarily fix the window.

"I'll wait till you get back," the chief told him.

The chief continued his search. In the guest bedroom closet he laughed when he saw mannequins dressed as regular people. *What the hell are those for?* he wondered? *I knew he was fucking strange.* Dan had some strange quirks, but this was bizarre. *Halloween maybe?*

His investigation revealed nothing more relating to 'The Club'. Wherever Dan hid his money, it seemed it would stay hidden; for now anyway.

While searching the house for Dan, Reggie came across what appeared to be a spare house key on the backside of the basement door. He retrieved it and kept it in case he needed to come back later.

Within ten minutes Jessie returned to put a wood plate over the broken window. It only took a few minutes and he was done. The chief locked up the house and they both left.

CHAPTER 30

Back at the office Reggie called the judge and briefed him on the days' events. They both had a good chuckle over the mannequins. The judge was pleased the chief had found the computer file, erased it, and found the notebook. They agreed that the chief should send out a missing person broadcast to law enforcement agencies and the press. They now needed any help they could get to find Dan.

"What do you think about opening back up?" asked the judge.

"I can't be sure, and I have no proof, but my money says Dan is dead. There was no indication he went anywhere. Everything is in place at his house, so I guess I'm in favor of it."

"All right, I'll notify June to open back up. Just let me know immediately if anything develops."

***

It was early evening and the chief was at home enjoying a beer and a cigar when he remembered the envelope containing Dan's Last Will and Testament. He pulled the Will and the computer disk from his jacket and sat looking at the envelope for several minutes. Should he read it? He couldn't contain his curiosity and he tore it open. Another envelope was inside the folded will. Typed on the outside of the face of the envelope, "TO BE OPENED ONLY BY THOMAS A. PERRY".

Reggie scanned the will. Dan had left everything he owned to Thomas A. Perry, June Perry's son. *What the hell,* he wondered? *Why would Dan leave everything to June's son?*

He opened the smaller envelope. It contained several paragraphs that astounded him. A secret, kept from everyone all these years, the letter read:

"Thomas, if you are reading this I have departed from this world. Do not let anyone read this letter. I don't know if your mother told you, but I am your biological father. We decided long ago to keep it a secret from everyone, but that I would help by paying child support for you, which I did and continue to do so. I know I haven't been a real father to you and I apologize for that and hope to make it up to you.

I want you to have the best education possible to give you a head start in life. In the basement of my house, now your house, go to the wall that has a green metal cabinet in front of it. Pull the cabinet away and you will find a metal plate attached to the wall. Unscrew the plate and you will find my life savings in cash. Do with it what you will, but I hope you will use it for a good education. Good Luck in the future. Love, Your Father, Dan"

The chief couldn't believe his good fortune! Dan was handing him his entire life savings, and he didn't even have to look for it! Now all he had to do is get back into the house and retrieve the money. He complimented himself on finding and keeping the key to the house he had found behind the basement door.

This will be a piece of cake, he thought to himself. He thought about whether he should go surreptitiously at night or confidently during the day on official business.

He decided he would go during the day. If anyone asked, since he was Dan's friend and Dan had no *known* family, he appointed himself caretaker until Dan returned or was found. He would collect his mail, pay his bills and watch over the property. This would give him legitimate opportunity to be at the house as much as he wanted. He also needed to find Dan's checkbook or bank statements and his credit card numbers so he could find out if any of them had been accessed. If they hadn't, it would tend to show that something had happened to him, would confirm his suspicions that he was dead, and it would be safe to take the cash. If the accounts had been accessed, he would have to leave things as they were for the time being.

The next morning about nine, the chief went to the house and let himself in. Picking up all of the newspapers on the front lawn, he brought them inside, and set the thermostat down to fifty-five degrees. He rummaged through the drawers in the desk for bank books, check books and credit card accounts. In the center drawer he found credit card statements from the prior month and checkbook and savings account statements from the Bank of Cripple Creek. He copied the account numbers and replaced the documents. Now he could check to see if any account had been accessed or used.

Reggie locked the house up and went over to the bank. Sandra was just arriving as the chief pulled up.

"How's everybody doing, Sandra?" The chief knew everyone was still upset about Norma's homicide.

"About as well as can be expected. It's put quite a load on me for now, having to work all these extra hours," she responded.

"I have a special request, Sandra. It's official, so let me know if I need to provide you with anything."

"What do you need?"

"Our former mayor, Dan Comeau, has been missing for over a week now. Nobody knows what happened to him. He was headed to the Springs in the snowstorm we had last week, and no one has seen or heard from him since. I have his account numbers; I just need for you to see if there has been any account activity in the past week. I have to check his charge accounts also, but they're not yours."

"Sure. I can do that. Come on in my office with me."

Sandra unlocked her office and Reggie followed her in. "I still get spooked coming in here. Even though everything has been cleaned up, repainted, new carpet and draperies, I still get a bad feeling every morning when I open."

"You're probably going to feel that way for awhile," said the chief trying to comfort her. "It's pretty natural in these circumstances to feel that way."

Sandra flipped the switch on her computer and waited for it to boot up. She logged on and asked the chief for the account numbers, which he gave.

"No activity on either account, Chief."

"Okay, that's all the info I needed. Thanks for the help. I'm still trying to trace him."

The chief went to his office and called Dan's credit card companies. After much numerous call transfers and rerouting of his call, he was able to get the fraud division of the companies to call him back. After checking, it was determined there had been no activity on either of his cards in the past week. The chief asked the companies to call him if and when there was any activity on the cards—which they agreed to do.

Now, the chief was satisfied that Dan was not coming back. Something had happened to him, they just didn't know what yet. Time would probably tell. But for now the chief felt he was free to find the cash that was stashed in Dan's house and relieve him of that burden.

The chief didn't know if he was going to tell Bill about June's son. He would have to divulge the Will and that would lead to the money. Maybe he would split the money with the judge; that way he could cover him if anything ever came up about it. Maybe.

***

Reggie waited until the next day to go back. He stopped at the station first to see if there were any messages from the credit card companies. Nothing. He was so excited he could hardly contain himself. Would there be the same amount of money that was notated in the computer file? He was like a kid at Christmas.

At noon, the chief told his secretary he was going out to lunch and to check on Dan's house. He headed directly over to the house. When he arrived, he grabbed the screwdrivers he had brought with him from his house and picked the newspaper up off the front lawn. He unlocked the front door and went inside. It was a little nippy in the house since he had turned the temperature down the day before and he shook off a chill. He opened the basement door and flipped on the light switch. Reggie went down the old wooden stairs that creaked with each step and looked around at the hundred-year-old stone foundation. Boxes were piled high in parts of the basement with old furniture stacked in other areas. A musty smell permeated the whole basement reminding him of his grandmother's house when he was a child. He found the green metal cabinet against the far wall and pulled the cabinet away. There was the plate, just as Dan had described in the letter.

His hands were shaking as he unscrewed the four Phillips-head screws holding the plate in place. The plate fell away, and there in the hole dug out of the stone and mortar were two large metal boxes. The chief pulled them out. They were heavy. He opened the steel lids and found stacks of banded hundred dollar bills in ten thousand dollar bundles. "Five, ten, twenty," he counted, "twenty-three." There were twenty-three bundles of ten thousand dollars, two hundred and thirty thousand dollars. *Holy shit*, he thought, *the jackpot!* He sat and looked at the cash, then recounted it twice.

Reggie grabbed an empty box he found in the corner of the basement and placed all of the money in it. He would cover the box with old newspapers, take it out to his car and place it in the trunk.

While replacing the plate, he suddenly stopped. *What if there are other copies of the will, possibly with a lawyer*, he thought? *They would suspect the money had been stolen if it was all gone. But would they suspect anything if he left some there? Say, fifty thousand? Naw, that's too much for a kid. Thirty thousand, that would do.*

He removed the plate, put thirty thousand back in one of the boxes, three bundles of ten-thousand, replaced the box and screwed the plate back on. He moved the cabinet back in place and placed the empty box in the cabinet.

The chief went back upstairs with his newfound treasure, turned the lights off and gathered up all the old newspapers he had brought in the past few days spreading them over the cash. He watched outside for a minute to make sure no one was watching and then carried the box out to the car and placed it in the trunk.

What a great lunch, he thought! Now he had to go home and dump the money off before going back to work. The chief had his special hiding place also, but it was a little more secure than the place Dan had. He had installed a large floor safe in his house about five years ago, but it had filled up with cash, all hundred-dollar bills. He recently installed another one, twice the size of the first. Now this one would be near capacity also. Tough problem to have, but he'd deal with it.

CHAPTER 31

The judge was waiting for June's Thursday night visit when Reggie called.

"What's up, Reggie?" Bill ask.

"I've got some info for you; wanted to come over for a few minutes."

"Make it quick, I'm expecting June and fixing supper. What's so important? Can't it wait until tomorrow?"

"I suppose so. It's not going anywhere," the chief replied. He was anxious to tell Bill about his good fortune and had decided to split some of the cash, but not all of it. He was going to tell the judge he found eighty thousand and give him half. If anything came up about the cash, forty thousand ought to be enough for the judge to cover his ass.

"Good, I'll talk with you tomorrow. Bye."

"See you tomorrow, Bill."

The judge waited for June to arrive.

***

June was on her way to the judge's house taking County Road One to Cripple Creek Mountain Estates where Bill lived as she did every Thursday night. There were several hairpin turns on the road heading out of town and a steep drop in elevation with several switchbacks. June was hungry, the judge had promised Veal Parmesan tonight and she had skipped lunch anticipating the meal. Her mouth watered just thinking of the feast Bill would be fixing for her, and he was a great chef. This was her night out, a night she could enjoy someone else fixing supper for her.

***

June never saw the pickup truck cross the road in front of her until the last second on the hairpin turn of the narrow two-lane road. It hit her head-on. She hadn't had time to react. Her car was totaled; the front end completely mangled, the windshield, driver and passenger windows broken out, the engine partially driven back into the passenger compartment. The airbag deployed protecting her upper body, but June was unconscious and pinned in the wreck. The truck that hit her had veered off the road after the collision into a ditch on the opposite side of the road. The driver of the truck was semi-conscious but his vehicle only had front-end damage as it had a large winch and frame on it.

Also going down the hill about a hundred and fifty feet behind June was the pastor, Brian Gray, driving his older Ford Explorer that was always breaking down. He was heading to a meeting with the pastor of the Open Air Chapel near the Mountain Estates to talk about a joint early morning Christmas service.

Brian pulled up behind June's car, put his flashers on and jumped out. He recognized June and quickly checked her vitals finding her unconscious but alive. It looked as if she may be trapped in her car. He then checked on the driver of the truck. He was coming to and moaning very loudly. Brian could smell an odor of booze emanating from the truck.

Brian knew a cell signal on this stretch of road was hit or miss. He looked at the phone; it had only one bar. He dialed 911 as he hailed down a passing car heading up the hill towards Cripple Creek.

"911. What is your emergency?"

"There's a head-on collision just south of Cripple Creek on Teller County Road One," the pastor hurriedly said.

The cell signal gave out. He didn't know if the entire message got through. He asked the driver of a passing vehicle, who said they had a cell phone, to call the police station as soon as they received a good signal, as he didn't know if his call was completely received by the 911 dispatcher.

Brian stayed with June and the other driver while he waited for the ambulance to arrive. He tried to comfort the truck driver with his assurances. June was still unconscious. It seemed like forever to Brian, but a short time later he could hear the scream of sirens heading his way.

The Cripple Creek Police cruisers were the first to arrive, followed closely by an ambulance, two fire engines and a rescue unit. The ambulance crew tended to the truck driver first, while the rescue crew, along with the fire crews, went to work on June's car, trying to cut her out of her car with power saws and pry bars.

The police officers took a statement from Brian, the only witness, directed traffic, called for two tow trucks, and started the accident paperwork.

"How is the librarian?" Brian asked one of the officers.

"I don't know. She's still unconscious and they are just now getting her out, but she looks to be in pretty bad shape. She's going to be flown to the hospital. They've already called for the life flight."

Brian stayed around until June was extricated from her vehicle. The other driver was treated at the scene as he refused to go to the hospital for any further treatment. The officers administered some field sobriety tests, then promptly arrested the truck driver for driving while under the influence of alcohol.

The tow trucks were hooking up the two vehicles and Brian took one last look at June's car before leaving. He saw her purse and coat still in the car.

He approached one of the officers. "Is it alright if I take June's personal items out of the car? I know her and don't want to see her things destroyed or stolen. Everything will get wet if it rains or snows, and I'm sure she will be in the hospital for awhile."

"Sure, go ahead, Pastor," stated the officer. "I'll let her know you have her things and I'll put it in the report. I'm sure she'll trust you. Just let me know what you take out for inventory purposes"

Brian grabbed her purse and coat from the floor of the passenger side front seat. He noticed a closed box on the floor of the back seat, some unopened mail addressed to June,, and some library books on the rear floor. He grabbed everything he observed that could be destroyed by water or snow, showed them to the officer, who inventoried them, and then placed them in his car to take home until he could get them to her.

CHAPTER 32

The judge dialed June's cell phone several times. She was almost an hour late, the supper he had prepared was getting colder by the minute, and he was getting hotter by the minute. There was no answer on her cell and it was going directly to voice mail. He called her house and Thomas told him she had left about an hour ago to join him for supper at his house.

Bill told him not to worry, there was probably a logical explanation and he would find out where she was. But the judge was worried. The mayor had disappeared out of thin air and now June was missing.

Bill called the chief. If anyone knew anything, he would.

"Hello, Bill," Reggie answered.

"Reggie, now June is missing," the judge said excitedly. "She was supposed to be here an hour ago. I called her house and Thomas told me she left to come here over an hour ago."

"Whoa, Bill. Calm down. I'm sure we can find out where she is. I'll call you back"

"All right, make it as quick as you can."

The chief called the station and asked if there had been any accidents in the past hour. He was told of the head-on crash on Teller One, involving June and a drunk driver.

"How is she? Where is she?" The chief was getting keyed up.

"They put her on a life-flight chopper to the Springs about a half hour ago. Her status right now is unknown."

"Has anyone notified her family?" he asked knowing her kids would have to be told, and someone would need to be found to take care of them.

"Don't know, Chief, you can talk to the officer if you want."

"No, I'll be at the station in a few minutes. Meanwhile, see if you can find out what her condition is before I get there."

"Ten-four, Chief, see you in a few."

Twenty minutes later Reggie arrived at the station. He went directly to the Sergeant-in-Charge and asked for a status report. Sergeant Majors was working an overtime shift.

"June is in serious but stable condition at Memorial Hospital in the Springs. She has a concussion, a compound fracture of her right leg, two broken ribs and several lacerations on her legs and head. Other than that, she's in perfect condition."

The chief glared at Majors, "That's not funny. June's a personal friend of mine. What about the kids, any relatives around?"

"Sorry, Chief. They have an aunt and uncle who are coming up from Woodland Park to get them. That's all taken care of."

"Good, I'll be in my office."

He went upstairs to call the judge.

"Bill, I've got some bad news. June was in an accident on her way to your house. A pickup truck driven by a drunk driver crossed the road by one of the hairpin turns and hit her head-on. She was airlifted out, but she's going to be all right as far as we know. They said she's in stable condition for now"

The chief then detailed her injuries to him, more information of the accident and that her kids were being cared for. He was going to do his best to make sure the drunk driver was hung out to dry.

"Reggie, there is one more thing that needs to be taken care of," the judge stated hesitantly as he didn't know what exactly to tell the chief. He couldn't tell him June was supposed to have his DVD's, no one else knew about them beside June and him. But the money, she also delivered everyone's split to him with the disks for him to dole out.

"What's that?"

"Did anyone take June's personal stuff out of the car? There was probably some cash she was bringing me to split up. We don't want it or her things stolen from the impound lot or junkyard."

"I'll see what I can find out and take care of things. Talk to you tomorrow."

The chief got the name of the towing company from the accident report. He would get June's possessions from the car the next day. There was nothing else he could do tonight, so he went home.

***

Bill was deeply upset about June's accident and couldn't eat the supper he had prepared for the two of them. He cleaned the kitchen, put everything away, and decided to watch and catalog more of his DVD's. June had been delivering about 30 disks per week and he was about two weeks behind in viewing and cataloging them. He had to get the disks that he hoped were still in June's car, they couldn't afford anyone watching them or even knowing they existed. He also had to get the money that was surely with the DVD's. He would have to go get all of the DVD's and money himself tomorrow.

The judge went to his hidden library and pulled out three DVD's from a box June had dropped off several weeks before. He plugged the first one into the DVD player, labeled Room 3-Blaze. He loved watching Blaze, one of his favorite girls.

About an hour later the next DVD, Room 1-China Doll, was loaded into the DVD player and started. Halfway thru the DVD he paused the disk, something was wrong. China Doll had been deep in conversation with a man they knew as the Colonel. She appeared to be very upset. The Colonel pushed her and she smacked him in the face. He threw a large manila envelope at her, lay down on the bed and appeared to go to sleep. A half hour later she woke him up and he left. "What the hell is going on?" he thought out loud.

He backed up the DVD, turned the volume up and listened intently.

"You stupid Chink bitch, you picked a hell of a place to make the last meeting. You didn't check for cameras. We were on video, on full display at the bank. They recorded everything," he said clenching his teeth. "You forced me to have to get the recording."

"What do you mean, I forced you to get the recording?" China Doll asked getting in the Colonel's face.

"What don't you understand?" he yelled pushing her out of his face, " I had to get the CD and destroy it. Don't you get it? We can't be seen together; especially me giving you the packet of information. It could cost both of us our lives. I *had* to get the recording."

She thought for a moment and recalled the news reports of the murder at the bank weeks before. "You were the one? You were the one that killed that innocent lady at the bank?" She slapped the Colonel in the face. "Stupid! You stupid! They will not like this in Denver!"

"Here," he said throwing a manila envelope at her, "Give this to your Chink friends and tell them I want my money. Yeah, they may not like it, but they'll understand it. It's not like they've never killed anyone." He took off his shoes and went and lay down on the bed. "Wake me up in half an hour."

China Doll folded the envelope and stuffed it in her oversized purse. She turned the TV on, made herself a cup of tea, and stared at the television for the next half hour when she walked over and shook the Colonel. He got up.

"Next time, do your due diligence. Find another place that's secure. I didn't find it very exciting killing someone either. I did what had to be done." He put his shoes on and left the room.

***

"What the fuck?" yelled the Judge putting his hand on top his head. "Holy shit! No,no,no! This can't be!" He played the video over and over. He still couldn't believe what he was watching and hearing. His hands were shaking. No one would believe him if….he could tell anyone. He absolutely couldn't.

He recognized what he was watching…a murder confession, and a traitor selling and delivering military secrets to the Chinese. Either one was devastating in itself, but both together?

"Could it get any worse?" he thought to himself. He had to tell someone, but whom? He should give the disk to the CBI or FBI. No, then his world would change forever; would come to an end, no more Club, no more money, no more DVD's, probably no more freedom. He visualized himself entering the federal prison in Canon City, 30 miles to the south. A judge in prison? No way! He had to keep this to himself. No one could know.

What this DVD contained was nuclear. It had explosive data that would change the lives of many people. He couldn't let it out, but it had to be kept. It would take very special safekeeping. If anything ever happened to him, it could be his "Get-Out-of-Jail-Free-Card."

CHAPTER 33

Agent Spencer White had returned to Denver after the crime scene at the bank had been processed. The next few days would be spent interviewing witnesses, employees and customers. The only problem he had was...there were no real suspects. The labs processed the disk that held the images of the bank robbery and murder of Norma Santiago. Multiple prints were lifted throughout the bank as they expected, but it would take awhile to match them to any prints on file. He really didn't expect the prints to provide any leads; they would only help if a suspect surfaced.

Spencer attended the autopsy the next day and retrieved another bullet. It appeared to be a .38 caliber, which was buried in Norma's head, along with several DNA samples. The bullet appeared to be in good condition. All were bagged and tagged for evidence and chain-of-custody. The samples of blood taken from several surfaces at the crime scene at the bank, along with the samples from the autopsy, and the bullets, were sent to the FBI crime lab in Washington for processing. They would try to match the bullet up to any other known crimes or samples on file.

The DVD proved to be invaluable. That afternoon, the lab brought Spencer multiple pictures of a white male, approximately forty-five to fifty years old, wearing a blue baseball type cap, white jacket, black jeans, sunglasses, black gloves, and carrying a revolver with a silencer. The disk did not record an actual video, but a frame-by-frame picture, approximately one second apart.

Spencer viewed the stack of eight-by-ten pictures on his desk processed from the disk. The suspect had entered by the front door, probably by knocking on it until Norma came to open it, the agent believed. The next frames showed the suspect with a gun at Norma's back, her arms partially raised, leading him over to the drive-up window. The suspect then loaded an empty coin bag with the overnight deposits. In the next group of photos, Norma appears to lead the suspect to the manager's office, unlocks the door and leads the suspect in. There was no camera in the office, but a camera in the lobby partially captured the suspect opening the cabinet that held the DVD recorder. Spencer assumed he was removing the disk. As the man started to exit the room, he turned and went back in. Although there was no one in the frames, the time sequence on the next several pictures matched the time the alarm came into the police department. Not in the camera's view, this would be when Norma was executed, probably when she was caught triggering the alarm by pushing a button under the lip of her desk. The suspect then came out of the office, closed the door behind him, and fled the bank out the front door with the disk and coin bag in one hand and the gun in the other. An outdoor camera captured him running away from the bank to the south, and that was the end of the photos.

Spencer believed there was more to the robbery. He had not seen a bank robbery before where the only money taken in the heist was the night deposits, as most of those tended to be checks. Was the guy an amateur, or had the suspect intended to take more, only to be scared away by the alarm Norma set off? Spencer had to know. He asked the lab for the complete video, and watched it entirely from the beginning to the end, approximately twenty hours. It was tedious and boring, watching all twelve cameras sequences each for twenty hours.

Spencer knew it wouldn't be unusual for a thief to case a bank before pulling off a robbery. Maybe he would get lucky and see a full view of the suspect without the glasses and hat.

Hours and hours were spent looking at each and every person who entered the bank. None of them fit the description entirely, but a couple came close. He decided to look through the video one more time. While fast-forwarding through the nighttime portion, which basically showed an empty bank, Spencer saw a flash of two vehicles in the parking lot next to the bank.

Could that be anything, he asked himself? He rewound the video and played it forward in slow motion. Two cars, a black Pontiac Grand Am and a white Mazda 626, had pulled into the lot at about eleven-forty. A male, who could possibly fit the description of the suspect, got out of the trailing vehicle and into the Mazda. About a minute later, he went back to the Pontiac, but he stalled, looking directly at the bank camera. He then left.

Spencer wondered what he had. Could it be related? It may not. It might just be a romantic tryst being setup, but the subject staring at the camera bugged him. He asked the lab for a blowup of that frame and one of the frames of the suspect in the robbery. He needed a facial and a full body blowup on both frames.

Later in the evening he received the photo blow-ups. The agent compared the photos. Different clothes-- different quality of photos. One was close, one far away.

He also requested his office printout all owners in Colorado of the type and year of vehicles in the photo. He knew that would take a little longer to obtain.

The next morning, Spencer drove the two hours south to Cripple Creek with several copies of his two photos and went to the bank to see if any of the employees could identify the male suspect.

At the bank, he had no luck; no one could identify the man. They couldn't even say they had seen him before.

He stopped at the police station to see Reggie and was taken upstairs to his office.

***

"Hello, Chief."

"Agent White, nice to see you again," the chief said getting up from behind his desk and extending his hand. He was lying of course. "I hope you've some news for us. Any leads?"

He pulled out copies of the photos and handed them to the chief.

"Hopefully. I'd like for your men to circulate these photos. See if they can find anyone that can identify the suspect in the bank photo. The second photo, I don't really know if it's related, but it may be the same person. It was taken around eleven-thirty the night before in the lot next to the bank."

Reggie scanned the photos. The photo of the suspect in the bank looked strangely familiar, but he couldn't place him. He didn't say anything to Spencer about his suspicions.

"Consider it done. I'll let you know if we get any hits."

Again, the chief just wanted to get rid of the Fed as soon as possible.

"These photos are our only leads as of the moment. We're generating a list of everyone who owns the type of vehicles in the second photo and I'll have that pretty soon. We can look at that next and start interviewing the owners. It might just be a harmless liaison. We'll see. I have also sent the bullet from the victim and all the DNA samples to our lab in Washington for analysis and comparison. I don't expect anything back very soon though."

"Well, let me know if we can do anything more for you," the chief stated extending his hand, hoping the Agent would take the hint and leave.

"Have a good day, Chief." Spencer shook the chief's hand, exited the office and went downstairs out to his car. He was hungry. On the way to Cripple Creek he had stopped at McDonalds and grabbed a sausage biscuit and orange juice, but now his stomach was growling. He decided to stop at Ralf's Breakroom, the only place in town he was familiar with, for a quick coffee and sandwich.

Spencer seated himself at the bar of Ralf's, and the bartender, Ted, brought him a menu. "Hey, aren't you that FBI guy that was here a while back?" asked Ted.

"Yeah, that's me," replied Spencer--obviously annoyed. He just wanted to get something to eat.

"Did ya catch the guy that robbed the bank and killed the woman yet?"

"No. How did you know it was a guy?" asked Spencer suspiciously.

"I have my sources," Ted replied, seemingly playing with the agent.

"No one has that information yet, but *you* do?"

"I'm just kidding. I didn't know; it just seems that most bank robberies are by men."

Spencer wasn't amused, but he observed a fresh cut notch in the beam above the bar.

"Did you cut another notch there, Ted?" Spencer asked pointing to the beam above the bar.

Ted looked above the bar, "I didn't even see that. It wasn't there yesterday."

Spencer panned the menu, "I'll have a coffee, a glass of water and a cheeseburger with the works."

Ted was still looking at the notch. "Okay, coming right up. Cream and sugar, right?"

"You got it." Spencer pulled out copies of the photos he'd brought from Denver and studied them in the dim light.

Ted brought over a setup, coffee, and some cream and sugar.

Spencer pushed the photos towards Ted. "You know a lot of people around here, ever seen this guy before?"

Ted looked at the photos for a couple seconds. "Can't say I have. That the guy?"

"Yes, but I don't know about that one," he said pointing to the parking lot photo, "It may be unrelated."

"Well, good luck finding the scumbag. He deserves to be burnt."

Spencer had his lunch and headed back to Denver.

CHAPTER 34

Pastor Brian missed the meeting with the pastor of the Open Air Church because of June's accident, but was able to contact him, explain the incident, and reschedule it for the next week. He was glad he was following June when the collision occurred and was able to help. He may have saved her life.

Brian grabbed all of June's effects he had taken out of her car and brought them into his house. His arms were full as he walked up the steps and he kicked at the bottom of the screen door. Christine came quick, opened the door and helped him with his load. He placed everything on the kitchen table.

"What in the world is all of this?" she asked.

"June was in a head-on accident out on Teller One. They had to cut her out of her car, so I gathered everything in her car that could be stolen or damaged by the weather. The police have a list of what I took." He related the rest of the details of the accident and aftermath to her.

"Is she okay?" Christine asked.

"I don't know. She was life-flighted out to the Springs. We'll probably have to wait until tomorrow to find out."

Brian excused himself for a few minutes to use the restroom. When he came back to the kitchen table, Christine had pulled a couple of DVD's out of the box. There were about twenty of them altogether, in plastic DVD cases, and they were all very similar, bearing white labels with handwriting on each label.

"Look at this, are these library DVD's?" she asked Brian. "This one says 'May 5th, Blaze, Room 3', this one 'May 6th, Blaze, Room 3', and so on. There are other DVD's with other names and dates also."

"Maybe they are from the school. She's the librarian and the city library is at the school."

"Could be, but it doesn't look like anything I've seen there."

"Well, I've had about enough excitement for the night, I'm going to bed," Brain said.

"I'll be there shortly, I have to finish cleaning up the kitchen."

Brian went upstairs to bed while Christine unloaded the dishwasher and cleaned the stove. She kept looking at the disks as if they were calling her, beckoning her to look at them. Curiosity finally got the best of her. She picked up the disk marked 'May 5th, Blaze, Room 3 and put it in the DVD player. She pushed PLAY.

At first all she saw was a bedroom that appeared to be decorated with Victorian era furniture and furnishings. As the DVD ran, a red-headed young woman, attired in Victorian garb came into view with a distinguished looking older gentleman, though his clothing was of modern day. They were laughing and hugging at first, which then became hugging and kissing. Christine believed she was watching a scene from a play at the Butte Opera House where a theater group performed melodramas downtown year round. Many of them were historic dramas. She was about to turn the video off when the gentleman started removing the lady's clothing and fondling her breasts.

Christine gasped, her eyes wide, her hands covering her mouth in shocked disbelief. She repeatedly jabbed at the remote control several times to stop the disk and sat staring at the blank television screen. She knew that couldn't possibly be a scene from a melodrama production; this was pornographic material.

Now, what was she going to tell her husband? Her curiosity had gotten the best of her and now she would have to explain that to her husband. She didn't want to, but she knew she had no choice. If the librarian, who was with her child at school everyday was into pornography, the school had to know. This was not something that would be tolerated by the community.

Christine slowly climbed the stairs to the second floor imagining what Brian was going to say. He would scold her for watching the video, but then hold back the criticism when she tells him what is on the disk. Then what?

"Brian, wake up. You have to see something," she said shaking him.

"What? What are you talking about?" Brian had already fallen into a deep sleep.

"I have to tell you something you're not going to like, but you'll be glad I did after you see what I found." There, she had gotten it out.

"Christine, what in the world are you talking about?"

"I watched one of the disks."

"What disks?" Brian still wasn't fully awake.

"The ones you brought home!"

"Oh, those. Christine, you shouldn't have messed with those, they aren't ours."

"I know, I know, but you have to come see it."

"Why? Why now? I was sound asleep."

"They, they…, they're pornographic."

"They're what?" That woke him up.

"I thought I was watching a scene from a Melodrama, but then…," she stopped, "Just watch it."

"Okay, let's go see it."

They both went downstairs; Christine hit 'Play' on the remote.

"Watch."

***

Brian watched the DVD until Christine stopped it at the same place she stopped before. She didn't want to see what was on the rest of the disk. Brian was repulsed, but knew what he was watching. It was Samantha, the lady who came to see him. Was this evidence of the brothel? Was this the evidence he and the FBI had been looking for? Could the librarian be working at the brothel? Could June actually be involved? *No way!*

"Brian, isn't that the woman who came to see you?" asked Christine.

"Yes, it is."

"Well, what is she doing in this?"

Brian was stuck between a rock and a hard place. He still couldn't reveal what Samantha had related to him. "Christine, I can't tell you anything yet, but trust me, I'll explain everything to you when the time is right."

Brian couldn't watch any more of the disk, but he knew who would be more than happy to. Adam wouldn't have a problem with it.

It was late, but now that Brian was wide-awake, Adam was going to be also. He excuse himself, went into his office and called Adam at home.

"Hello, this better be good," answered Adam.

"Adam, this is Brian, sorry to bother you this late. I've got something you have to see."

"Oh, Brian. Sorry. What is it?"

Brian related the story of how he came into possession of the disks.

"Christine watched one of them. That's another story. Adam, but I think they are disks from the brothel.

"What? You got to be shit... You've got to be kidding me."

"I need you to watch the disk. We watched the first few minutes of it, but..."

"I understand. Say no more. Can we do this in the morning or..."

"Adam," Brian interrupted, "if this is what I think it is, there will probably be someone here in the morning to retrieve them."

"Yeah, you're probably right. Okay, I'll be over in a few minutes. Put the coffee on."

"Got it. See ya in a few."

Brain came back out to the kitchen. Christine had a puzzled look on her face.

"Brian, I wasn't trying to listen, but I heard you mention something about a brothel. What's going on?" she asked.

"Christine, have a seat. There's a lot going on you don't know about. I've had to keep you in the dark because you are the only one who knows who gave me the information. I didn't think it would be right for you to know what she told me, but now... I was also trying to protect you."

"Protect me?"

"The girl's name is not important, but she told me there was a brothel in town, she worked there, and wanted me to help her get out of it. I haven't heard from her since. She told me it might be dangerous for all of us just knowing about it, and if anyone ever found out what she had revealed to me, she would definitely be in grave danger. She was extremely scared and took a really big chance coming to see me."

"Poor girl. I hope she's alright."

"So do I, but I have no way of reaching out to her to find out."

"I took a chance and spoke to Adam about it in general terms. I asked him if he had ever heard anything about a brothel in town. It turned out the FBI was investigating the same thing, but they didn't know where it was or who was involved. Adam is their contact in town. The girl told me to be careful because prominent citizens and community leaders were possibly involved, but she couldn't or wouldn't name any names."

"Wow, no wonder you were so lost in thought and secretive sometimes. That's a lot to carry around. I really wondered what was bothering you."

"I'm sorry, but now you can see why I couldn't tell you about it. I didn't want you to worry, and as I told Adam before, I wanted us totally out of this mess. I didn't want anything to happen to you and Madison."

"And now I got us back into it."

"Well, the Lord must have different plans."

About twenty minutes later Adam arrived and greeted Brian and Christine. Christine prepared coffee while sheepishly relating to Adam her sin of snooping and what she found. She was embarrassed to admit what she did, but excited as to what she discovered.

"I thought you wanted completely out of all this, Brian," said Adam teasing Brian about their previous conversations.

Brian smiled, "I thought I did too, Adam, but the Lord just keeps bringing it back."

Brian brought Adam into the living room where the television and DVD' player were located, and started the video.

"We'll be in the kitchen, Adam."

"Okay, I understand. Let me check it out."

For about ten minutes Brian and his wife sat at the kitchen table waiting for Adam to join them. They sat silently looking at each other.

Adam stopped the DVD, came to the kitchen and sat down with them at the table.

"Well, I don't think there is any doubt what the DVD is, Brian. It's got to be from the brothel. Either that or someone is making pornographic home videos. Looking at the labels and the quantity of disks, though, I tend to think it is a brothel."

"It took ten minutes of watching to figure it out?" Brian asked, teasing Adam.

"Yeah, well I had to be absolutely sure."

"Where do we go from here?" asked Brian.

***

Adam was thinking he really wanted to see the rest of the disks, but he knew he couldn't say that in front of the pastor and his wife. Besides, time was short and he'd have a boner he wouldn't be able to hide. That would be embarrassing.

"I didn't recognize any of the people in the video, did either of you?"

Both shook their heads no.

"I'd like to keep one of the videos to pass on to the FBI, but if we do that, June may discover it missing. Any ideas?" asked Adam.

"How about copying one of the disks," Christine suggested.

"That would be the best thing, does anyone have another DVD recorder that we could borrow this late?" asked Adam. "All I have is DVD players at home."

"Not this late," said Brian, "not without raising questions."

"I've got an idea," suggested Adam, "Why don't I just download the disk to my computer, then I can burn another copy. I've go plenty of DVD's at the office.

"Sounds like a plan to me. Let's go for it," said Brian.

Adam left, went to his office with the disk and burned another DVD.

The recording took about two hours. When Adam returned they sat at the kitchen table discussing the possible ramifications for the librarian once the FBI received the recordings of the disks.

"I think you ought to take some photos of the other disks. We can't record the content of them all, but at least you could lay them out and get a picture of what the labels say," Christine said.

"Good idea Christine," said Adam, "let's spread them out on the table here and I'll get the my phone. It's in my jacket."

Adam went to get his phone while Christine and Brian took all the disks out of the box and spread them on the table. When they reached the bottom of the box, they found a bulky envelope. Christine pulled the envelope out and opened it. There, inside, was a thick bundle of hundred dollar bills.

She looked at Brian. She had never held so much money before.

"Count it," he said.

She sat down and started counting the bills.

Adam came in the kitchen and stared at the cash she was counting.

"Where did that come from?" he asked.

"It was in the bottom of the box, in an envelope," said Brian.

"Spread it out on the table and I'll get a photo of it along with the disks," said Adam.

There were one hundred of them.

"Ten-thousand dollars," she said.

It was after two in the morning when the entire picture taking was finished. They placed everything back in the box, envelope on the bottom, and disks on top.

"I'll make contact in the morning with the FBI, Brian, and give you a call after that."

"I'll be waiting."

CHAPTER 35

Reggie was at the police station around seven-thirty the next morning. He had to be in court this morning at eight-thirty to testify on a rape case he investigated six months earlier. He called the company that had towed June's car the night before and told them he was coming over to retrieve the personal affects of the owner.

He was told a gentleman who had witnessed the accident and knew the lady who was in the accident had taken everything out of the car the night before. This was all done with the permission of the officer investigating the accident.

The chief went downstairs and pulled a copy of the accident report and the accompanying officer's report. At the end of the statement, there in black and white, the officer had given Pastor Brian Gray permission to secure the personal items of June Perry.

Good, I'll have to thank him for taking care of her things, Reggie thought. There was no hurry to get the items; he could stop over after court.

***

At eight that morning the judge was also eager to retrieve June's possessions from her vehicle. He couldn't afford for anyone to see the disks, or even know they existed, even the chief. Plus, he had to get the money and distribute everyone's share; they would be expecting it.

Bill made his way to the police station in his specially equipped handicapped van. He hated driving, as all the controls were on his steering wheel. He never really drove enough to get used to the controls and tried to only drive locally. Whenever he had to go to the Springs or other places out of town, his other van was equipped for him as a passenger. He always had someone who would volunteer to drive.

Bill arrived at the police station and parked in the handicap space in front of the station. He was ready to take Reggie to the towing company to get June's personal items. He called the Chief and told him he was out in front of the station and asked him to come out and see him. Reggie complied with his request.

"What are you doing out this early?" asked the chief.

"I wanted to find out how June was and get her stuff. I might go down to the hospital today. She'll probably want her purse."

"Well, I just found out all her things are over at the pastor's house. He got them out of her car last night at the accident. I was going to get them after I got out of court later on."

The blood drained from the judge's head; he couldn't speak for several seconds as questions ran through his head. *Really? It had to be the pastor? What if he found the money? What if he looked at the disks?* He couldn't share his fears with the chief.

"What's the matter, are you all right?" asked Reggie.

"Yeah, I'm fine. I think June was bringing our money from you-know-where. I hope the pastor didn't go through her things. That amount of cash may be hard to explain." He hoped that explanation would satisfy the chief. "I'll stop over and get her things. I'll let you know if anything is missing."

"Okay, I doubt you'll have a problem. The pastor isn't going to take the money, so ease up. I have to get to court. I'll talk to you later."

The judge called the pastor's house as soon as Reggie left. Christine answered; he asked for Brian and she gave him the phone.

"Brian, this is Judge Tillis."

"Hello, Judge, How are you?"

"Very good, thank you. I am going down to see June this morning. She asked me to get her purse for her and I understand you pulled all of her things out of her car last night. Could I come by and get them?"

"Certainly. How is she?"

Bill didn't have any idea how June was. Right now he didn't care.

"She's doing better. I'll know more this afternoon when I see her."

"Great."

"Is it alright if I just honk when I come over, I don't have anyone with me. If you could bring her things out, I would appreciate it."

"No problem, Judge, we'll be waiting."

"Thank you, I'll be there in a few minutes."

The judge couldn't tell if they knew anything. It didn't sound like it.

He arrived at the pastor's house a few minutes later and Brian and his wife were waiting on their porch with the items. They opened the passenger door, placed the box of disks on the floor and the remaining items on the seat. Bill decided he would test them.

"What's in the box?" he asked.

Brian hated lying, but this would be an exception. "Don't know. Looks like DVD's. They were in the back seat of June's car. I just gathered everything I saw."

"I'm sure she appreciates everything you did for her. My thanks also."

"Glad to help. Tell her we wish her the best and we'll be praying for her."

Bill thanked them and left. He could see the disks were secure and hopefully the money would be in the bottom of the box. It didn't sound to him like they knew anything. He drove down the block and turned the corner. Opening the box, he pulled the disks out and found the cash on the bottom. Now he could call on June and let the chief know he had picked up the items. He felt a huge load lifted off his shoulders and breathed a sigh of relief.

***

As soon as the judge left, Brian was on the phone calling Adam.

"It was the judge that picked up June's things" he reported, "but I don't know if he knows about the disks and money. He asked me what was in the box that had the disks; acted like he didn't know anything about it."

"Judge Tillis, eh? Probably an act, but it's not up to us now. I'll be calling Denver soon and let them know what we have," said Adam.

"Yeah, that fits what I told you about what the girl told me, "there are prominent citizens and community leaders possibly involved."

"I know, so be careful," Adam stated.

***

Later that morning Adam notified his FBI contact, Agent Kemp, of June's automobile accident, their discovery of the disks, cash and the judge making the pickup of the items this morning.

"Unbelievable," exclaimed the agent, "this definitely gives us some leads."

"That's not all," stated Adam, "we made a copy of one disk for you and took photos of the rest of the DVD's on their kitchen table along with the cash. I have a disk for you with all that data on it. "

"I'll need that disk as soon as we can get it," said Kemp, "I'll arrange a meeting for the pickup. I'll call you back as soon as I can put it together."

"OK, I'll wait for the call."

***

At the same time Adam was calling Agent Kemp, Bill was calling June in the hospital. She was groggy, but awake. After asking her how she was and finding she was going to be in the hospital for a while he gave her the news about her car.

"June, I have the items that were in your car."

"Oh, good, I was worried about them," she responded slowly. "Did you find the special item in the bottom of the box?"

"Yes, I have that also. It was Pastor Brain who saw your accident. He's the one who called the police and rescue. He was able to retrieve all the stuff out of your car before it was towed. Did you know it was totaled?"

"I kind of figured it was. How did you get everything?"

"I told the pastor you asked me to get your purse and I told him I would get the rest of the things to you. I asked him what was in the box and he told me he didn't know, so I didn't think he looked at anything. If he ever asks, you requested that I get your items."

"Will do. What about my kids?"

"Your kids are fine, they're being taken care of by your sister."

"Good, come see me sometime. Take care of everything while I'm gone."

"I will. Get well soon and if you need anything, let me know."

"I will."

CHAPTER 36

Special Agent Brandon Kemp called Adam back a couple hours later.

"I'll be in Cripple Creek in a couple of hours to pick up the disk. I'm going to introduce you to another Agent that I want you to start coordinating things with down there. I'll explain everything that I can to you at that time. Can you meet us in a couple hours at Ralf's?"

"I think so, should Brian come too?"

"Sure, you can bring him. He's integral to the investigation and he's shown his mettle. I'd like to meet him."

"Good, say five o'clock then?" asked Adam.

"Perfect, see you then."

Adam called Brian and informed him of the meeting at five with the two agents. Brian said he could make the meeting and agreed that Adam would pick him up about quarter till.

***

At five o'clock Brian and Adam walked into Ralf's Breakroom and took seats at a corner table in the bar area, the most secluded table available, as the restaurant area was busy with dinner customers. They ordered coffee from Ted who brought their order.

"So, what brings you two in here today," ask Ted.

"We just wanted a cup of coffee where we could chat a bit," said Adam. He didn't want Ted hanging around when the agents arrived.

"Pastor, I'm surprised you're in the bar area, wouldn't you be more comfortable in the restaurant area?" asked Ted with a wink.

Brian was surprised at the question, but caught the wink, and came right back. "Sometimes we have to visit the dark areas of the world to find our lost sheep," he said to a smiling Ted. He knew Ted was teasing him, but Adam didn't see the wink and took it a different way.

"Could we just have some privacy, please?" asked Adam.

"Sure, enjoy your coffee," said Ted as he went back to the bar.

"He was just playing with me Adam, he's okay."

"I just didn't want him hanging around when the agents come in. They're going to stick out with their suits anyway, I don't need his big ears listening in on us."

A few minutes later, Agent Kemp came thru the front door. Adam waived him back to their table.

"Hello, Adam."

"Hi Brandon. Agent Brandon Kemp I'd like to introduce Pastor Brian Gray. Brian, Agent Kemp."

"Pastor, great to meet you. I hear you've been pretty busy lately helping us out," he said shaking Brian's hand.

"Nice to meet you too. Seems like it. I've wanted to get out of this mess for a while now. Adam keeps bringing me back in. I can't stay away from him."

The agent laughed.

"I thought there was another agent coming with you," said Adam.

"Oh, he'll be here in a couple minutes," replied Agent Kemp with a broad smile.

Ted came back to the table and asked the agent what he would like.

"Just a coffee, please, cream and sugar--and make it fast. I haven't got all day."

Brian and Adam looked at each other--they didn't expect the agent to be so rude.

Ted grabbed a cup of coffee for Kemp, and brought it back to the table. "Get your own cream and sugar," he told the agent and sat down at the table next to Kemp.

Adam was stunned at the lack of manners exhibited by the bartender. "We've always had a hard time getting good help in this town," he stated to Agent Kemp. "Ted, please excuse us." His voice was sterner now.

Ted was laughing; he couldn't hold it any longer.

Agent Kemp looked around the room and in a low voice spoke up, "Adam, Brian, I want you to meet Special Agent Steven Coats."

There was dead silence for a moment, and then Brian burst out laughing at the look on Adam's face. His jaw almost hit the table and you could have knocked him over with a feather.

"Excuse me, Brian," said Adam, "but, *no shit!*"

"Gentlemen, for this operation to continue working, you must keep this entirely confidential. If the disk contains what you've described, I won't be in my office much for a while. Steve will be your contact from now on. He can get in touch with me twenty-four seven. Here's Steve's cell number. Call him anytime you need to. We are getting closer, but the hard work is still to come. Agent Coats needs to keep working here and I'll need everyone's eyes and ears. You have to swear to me you won't breathe a word."

Both Adam and Brian nodded in agreement. Steve got up to go back to work.

"See you boys later," and in a lower voice said, "and please, keep calling me Ted."

"You guys watch each other's backs. Where's the disk?" asked Agent Kemp.

Adam produced the disk from inside his shirt. "Enjoy," he told the agent.

"You say this June Perry is in Memorial Hospital right now?" He asked.

"As far as I know," stated Adam, "Sounds like she got pretty beat up in the accident; several broken bones, cuts, etc. The judge said he was going down to see her this afternoon. I expect she will be in there for awhile."

"Either Steve, I mean Ted, or I will be in touch with you. I hope this disk gives us what we need. Where do you think the other disks are now?"

"The judge picked them up this morning when he got the rest of June's personal items. He acted like he didn't know what they were. He either took them to June or he still has them and the money," replied Brian.

Agent Kemp got up to leave. "Please stay here for a few minutes after I leave. It'll look better that way." He stopped at the bar, picked up the tab, had a few words with Steve, and left.

Brian laughed. Adam still looked like he was in a daze.

"Don't that take all?" said Adam looking over at Ted. "Well, what happens now?

"We go home and let them handle things," said Brian.

"That will be nice for a change, and don't call me in the middle of the night anymore," said Adam, hitting Brian on the shoulder.

"I told you I wanted out of this thing. It keeps coming back, just like a bad penny."

CHAPTER 37

Agent Kemp returned to Denver as fast as possible to review the disk given to him by Adam. He believed the DVD came from a brothel, but it would still be hard to prove it was in Cripple Creek or that June had anything to do with it. She could have been transporting the twenty disks for someone as a favor, or, she could be in it up to her neck. The cash and the labels on the DVD's tended to prove it was a very large operation.

He called Memorial Hospital to get the status of June. She was in fair, but stable condition. He was told she could talk, but was on an IV pain medication and may fall asleep at any time. He decided to let her rest for the night and see her tomorrow.

***

The next morning Agent Kemp met with the U.S. District Attorney for Denver. The attorney was briefed on the DVD in his possession and contents along with the other DVD's and cash. Kemp ask the D.A. for immunity for June if she cooperated fully with the investigation. They had no reason to believe at this point that June was involved in the espionage case they were investigating, but they didn't know for sure. It would be Kemp's job to find out. He got the approval for the immunity and further approval for a search warrant of June's house, car and office if he needed it.

From the D.A.'s office he went straight to Memorial Hospital in Colorado Springs. He found June still in the intensive care unit, but awake and alert. She was to be moved to a standard room that afternoon.

***

"Good morning June, how are you feeling this morning?" asked Agent Kemp.

"I feel like a truck rolled over me," June replied. She studied the agent, thinking he was too well dressed to be a doctor, but he could be. "Who are you?"

"I'm Special Agent Kemp with the FBI. I need to ask you some questions. Do you feel well enough?"

"About what?"

"In relation to a brothel we know is in operation in Cripple Creek. We have information that you have some part in it. That is what I am here to discuss with you." He didn't know for sure the brothel was in Cripple Creek, but decided to take a shot at it.

June was silent for a minute. She wasn't about to just give everyone up that easy. "Do I need a lawyer? I really don't know what you are talking about."

"June, I'm going to ask you to think about your kids. You can cooperate with us and keep your family together, or you can play stupid; we'll play rough, and you will go to jail for quite awhile. You make the choice, but I need you to make a decision now."

The Mayor, she thought. *They have Dan--he spilled his guts to the FBI. That son-of-a-bitch.*

She thought of her sons. She would die if anything happened to them or if she had to go to jail. She knew she was had, but, why would they need her information if they had Dan?

"Do you have Dan?"

"I'm not here to answer your questions, at least not yet. You have to make up your mind if you're going to answer mine."

June didn't answer.

"I will tell you I have watched some of the DVD's you had in your car. They were pretty revealing, in more ways than one."

"You mean the pastor watched them? The pastor did me in?"

"No, the pastor didn't watch them."

"Well, who did?"

"I can't tell you that right now. I need you to tell me if you are going to cooperate. This is a large-scale investigation and you can either get on the bus or get run over. As I said, it's your choice.

"Can I have some time to think it over?"

"Yes, you can have about two more minutes, then I'm walking out of here. I already have authorization for search warrants for your house, car and office at the library. I can also charge you with conspiracy to commit espionage. When I walk out of here, your life will change, and I can guarantee it won't be for the better."

"Espionage?" she yelled.

"Keep your voice down. Yes, espionage. I could give a flying shit about the prostitution and your whorehouse. I need other information."

"Can I get immunity from anything I tell you?"

"The U.S. District Attorney for Denver has authorized me to grant you immunity as long as you cooperate completely. The first lie or unreasonable memory loss you have will invalidate our agreement. It must be the truth and the *whole* truth. Do you understand? "

"Yes."

"I will have the agreement faxed here within the hour. I need you to sign it and we will begin. You will not call anyone and you are not to accept any calls until then. Do you understand?"

"Yes."

"In addition, you will not be allowed any visitors and you will not talk to anyone except medical personnel. I am placing a guard at your door. I'll be back with the agreement. I'm having your room phone deactivated, so you don't get any last minute ideas. Do you have a cell phone with you?"

"No, it was in my purse. Judge Tillis has it."

"Okay, I'll be back."

Agent Kemp called the hospital security and asked for an officer to be posted at her door and gave instructions that no one was to enter her room except medical personnel. He then contacted his office and asked for twenty-four hour protection and surveillance on her room by FBI agents.

CHAPTER 38

An hour later Agent Kemp returned to the hospital to see June with the offer of immunity paperwork and a tape recorder. She read and signed the offer, keeping a copy. Then the interrogation began and he turned on the tape recorder. He went over all the technical details that needed to head the recording, and then started the questioning.

"Okay June, I want you to remember your part of the agreement. No hedging or hiding anything. You must answer all questions truthfully and completely or the immunity is voided. Understand?"

"Yes."

"I want you to know I am going to be asking you questions that I already know the answer to, so I will know if you aren't being truthful. I am going to record our conversations. If I find you hedging on any answers or not being truthful, the District Attorney will throw the deal in the trashcan. Understand?"

"Yes."

Agent Kemp didn't want June to know he didn't know where the brothel was. That was the one thing he had to find out.

"June, first tell me about the brothel."

"What do you want to know?"

"Everything."

"We started the brothel about ten years ago. There were four of us, locally, who had the idea and decided to start the brothel. We each put in equal amounts of cash, but we still needed a larger investment to really make it great."

"How much did each of you put in?"

"A hundred-thousand. We also needed to start a dating service to bring only the best customers to the brothel."

"Where did you start the service?"

"We set up an office in the Springs and started advertising there and in Denver and Pueblo."

"Tell me about the investors."

"The judge told us he found three wealthy investors, but with the demand the rest of us would never know who they were. So, I don't know the names of those three, only the judge does."

"You mean William Tillis?"

"Yes, he is a very close friend of mine, this is very difficult," she slowly said.

"Just keep thinking about yourself and your kids. Besides the judge and yourself, who are the other two locals?"

"The police chief and the son-of-a-bitch ex-mayor, Dan Comeau. But I'm sure you already know about him."

"Ex-mayor?"

"Yes, he went missing awhile back, in November I think. He resigned just before that."

"That's a pretty good list of characters. Does anyone else local know about your activities?"

"Not as far as I know."

"Okay, go on."

"Anyway, we have about twelve girls working for us, about five on any given day."

Kemp wanted the location of the brothel. "What made you choose the location?"

"Well, when the casino went out of business, the bank took it over and eventually placed it up for auction. We bought it and opened the nightclub. We found the passageway to the rooms under the old

Homestead House. We thought it would be funny to have a real, working brothel under a historic brothel; kind of ironic you know."

"Tell me about Tillis."

"He's pretty much the big guy. He is also the boss of Marcos, our enforcer, who takes care of any rule violations and discipline matters. The judge gets all the money to distribute to the partners of 'The Club'."

"'The Club'?"

"That's what we call ourselves. The four of us and the other three whom I don't know. What's this about espionage? I don't know anything about that."

Kemp thought a moment. "I guess I can tell you a little. Your brothel is central to a major espionage investigation. That's all I can tell you right now. Like I said earlier, I can give a shit about the prostitution, that's not why we are here. The State of Colorado may have something to say about it, but I don't care. Tell me about the DVD's."

"The DVD's. When Bill, the judge, had his accident a few years back, he was unable to have sex anymore. He loved watching the girls though. He had his favorites. He had me hide cameras in all the rooms and video all the liaisons. No one knows about the DVD's except for Bill and me. We kept it a secret between us. I deliver them to him every Thursday night along with cash from the weeks take and he fixes me supper. He's a great chef. I was on my way to his place when that asshole crashed into me."

"Where does Tillis keep the DVD's?"

"They're at his house. He has a hidden room, he keeps them all logged and cataloged."

"So, all the DVD's are in one location right now?"

"Yes, all of them are at Bill's house."

"How many are there?"

"He's got over a thousand by now. I don't know exactly how many he actually has."

"How do we get in the brothel?"

"You have to have a special access card. I have it in my purse. It looks like a credit card. In the elevator, you slide the card in a special credit card type receiver and it will take you down. Otherwise you can only go up to the hotel."

"Do you have any documents, or anything relating to the brothel at your home or office, or hidden in your car?"

"No, everything is kept in my office at the brothel. The keys to my office in the brothel are in my purse."

"Do you have any Chinese nationals working at the brothel?

"Yes, China Doll. She's the only one."

"What is her real name?"

"Tao Yang. She's here on a student visa. She's worked for us for almost a year now."

"Where does she live?"

"All I know is somewhere here in the Springs. Her address would be in her personnel file in my office."

"Tell me about the chief, what role does he play in your group?"

"The chief is the chief. He does pretty much what the Judge Tillis tells him to do. He's the scare factor if we needed him to talk to anyone without using Marcos. He does background checks on our girls and customers before we let them in."

"Okay, that is all I need for now. I'm having you moved to a hospital in Denver where you'll be safe. You'll have a twenty-four hour guard there and be well taken care of. If you want to see your kids, let me know and I'll arrange to have them brought to you. For now, you will be incommunicado, you won't be able to talk to anyone."

"Great," she said sarcastically.

CHAPTER 39

Agent Kemp called Denver and requested an FBI team to raid the nightclub and brothel. He also needed two smaller teams to arrest and hold the chief and the judge. They had to occur simultaneously, he didn't want anyone to get tipped off. He gave them Tao's name and told them to check on her immigration status, find where she lived or anything else on her. All he knew was that she was supposed to be here on a student visa and possibly lived in the Springs.

He then called the D.A.'s office. He needed search warrants for the brothel, nightclub, the judge's house and cars, and the chief's house, office and vehicles. This was going to be a very large, complicated operation and very time consuming. Within three hours he was notified he had his arrest and search warrants.

He still needed an address on Tao. She was the priority; the key to their whole investigation. He wanted her found, brought in, and her place searched...right now. How could he find her? If they couldn't find an address, she would eventually come to work. But if they raided 'The Club', she would possibly find out and disappear. He couldn't chance that.

The judge, he seemed to be the key to the whole operation. First things first. He decided he would quietly bring in the judge and the chief while maintaining surveillance on the nightclub instead of raiding it immediately.

***

Two hours later, twelve agents from the FBI met Kemp at the Walmart parking lot in the Woodland Park. They brought the warrants with them, and he briefed them on their assignment. He assigned two agents each to pick up the judge and the chief and transport them to Denver. Neither of them were to know the other was also arrested. It was to be done 'quietly'. Two agents were assigned surveillance at the nightclub, and the other six were assigned searches, three at the judge's house and three at the chief's house. He would accompany the two agents arresting Bill.

It was late evening when they chose to arrive at the judge's house. The six agents climbed the back stairs and knocked on the door.

"Come in, it's open," yelled the judge.

Agent Kemp opened the door and he and the five other agents entered.

***

Bill had a bad feeling when he saw six suits.

"William Tillis?," asked Kemp as the judge wheeled his chair towards them.

"Who's asking," he demanded.

"Special Agent Kemp, FBI."

"Well, then, I suppose so. What do you need?" He didn't have a clue as to why six FBI agents would come to his house.

"I have an arrest warrant for you, Mr. Tillis. We are taking you to Denver. I also have a warrant here for the search of your premises and your vehicles."

"Let me see those warrants."

Kemp gave him the warrants to read. They were federal warrants. He had never seen federal warrants before.

"What's this about conspiracy and espionage?" he asked in a more moderated tone. He knew what they wanted, but couldn't understand why they would arrest him. The DVD had all the answers.

"We'll get to that later, but for now, I'm having these two agents transport you to Denver. You will be booked and processed and I will talk to you afterwards."

"You'll talk to me now," yelled the Judge. "I know what you're after. That little weasel, Dan, he just didn't live up to our expectations. What has he told you? If you want me to cooperate, you'll talk to me now."

"All right, Mr. Tillis, what do you want to tell me?"

"What exactly is it you're after?" Bill didn't want to give anything away and wanted to make sure he was on the right track.

"To make it short and sweet, Mr. Tillis, your little club. You are running a brothel, a criminal enterprise, where we believe espionage is taking place, where military secrets are being transferred to a foreign entity."

"Your looking for a military man, right?

"Yes."

"Handing over documents to the Chinese? Right?"

"Keep going."

"What if I could hand over the two that you want? Give you names. What if I could prove beyond any doubt who you are looking for, *and* show it to you on video? What if I could show you a murder confession by one of them on video?"

"Murder? That could help you quite a bit, I'm sure. Tell me about the murder," said Kemp.

"The bank robbery and murder you guys are supposedly investigating, Norma Santiago."

Kemp had heard about the murder and robbery, but he had no idea it would be tied into his investigation.

"You're saying the murder of Norma Santiago and the robbery is tied to our espionage investigation?"

"Yep, that's what I'm saying. I can give it all to you on a silver platter."

"Tell me about it."

"I will, after we work something out. If I'm going to hand these people over to you, there's going to have to be some quid-pro-quo here."

The judge was gambling that the Feds would bend, and kept a straight poker face. He knew there could be some negotiations here; he just didn't know how far he could push.

"What do you want? You know I have to get authorization for any deals, I can't authorize it myself."

"I know that. Make the call. I want the witness protection program with a new name and relocation, and complete immunity from federal and state prosecution. And since I'm throwing in the murder, which obviously you didn't know about, I also want immunity for my friends, the chief and June." Bill wasn't sure, but he figured they must be ready to arrest the chief and June along with him. Besides, if he were going to have to give full and complete information, he would have to tell them about June and the chief in the process.

Kemp hesitated. "What about the other four partners of your club?"

Bill was sure they had the old Mayor now; they knew how many partners were in 'The Club', and he had spilled his guts. "Let them hang, along with Dan,"

"I'll be back."

Kemp stepped outside to call the D.A. She was the only one who could authorize any deals and she would have to contact the District Attorney in Colorado Springs regarding any state or county charges that they may want immunity for.

It was after hours and he had to wait for the D.A. to call him back. While he was waiting for that call, he called the agents that were at Reggie's house and told them not to transport him to Denver yet. They could do the searches, but to hold Reggie there until they heard from him again.

Meanwhile he still had to search the house. Maybe he would get lucky and not have to give a deal to the old codger. He instructed the other agents to go ahead with their search.

"Where's the hidden room with all the video DVD's?" asked Kemp.

"Well, I suppose I can tell ya that. I don't want you tearing up my house looking for it."

He wheeled his chair and motioned for them to follow over to the far side of the living room and pointed to a floor-to ceiling bookcase.

"Pull it out, it's hinged."

Inside, the room was lined from waist high to the floor on three sides with shelves containing DVD's. June had been right, there were well over a thousand of the DVD's stuffed into a space just large enough to get a wheelchair in and out. Each DVD was labeled and cataloged with dates, room numbers and names.

The judge was puzzled. Dan didn't know anything about his library or the recording system at the brothel. The only other person was June. Did they already have her? Do they already have Dan *and* June? Would June have given him up? She was the only one with a family; he supposed she would be easy picking. Or was his phone and house bugged? He would have to be more careful *next* time.

"You can look in there all you want, take your time, boys. There are about twelve hundred DVD's, each about, oh, say, five to six hours long. So that's about six to seven thousand hours of video to review. The segment you will be looking for is about, oh, say, three minutes long. Hope you don't miss it, you'd have to start all over again."

The agents were looking at each other. *Who was this asshole? And he's a judge?*

"Then again, there's nothing to say the video is in there. You wouldn't even know if was there and you missed it, or it wasn't in there to begin with. You might have to view all the DVD's four or five times before you would know. I might have put that DVD somewhere else for safekeeping; maybe for a situation just like this."

Bill was on a roll and was actually having a little fun with the Feds. They had invaded his privacy, his private collection of his girls, and he certainly didn't like it.

"Go ahead and search the rest of the house," instructed Kemp. He didn't like wasting time, and they already had a long search ahead of them.

About twenty minutes later, the D.A. returned his call from a restaurant in Denver. He briefed her on the information the judge had given him and what the judge wanted in return. Since the investigation had been going on for almost a year and they had everything almost ready to close, Kemp requested they give him what he asked for. Besides, he could give a shit about the whorehouse and the gambling. From what June had told him, Kemp didn't believe the judge nor the chief were involved in what they really cared about...the NORAD documents being transferred to a foreign government.

"All we really want is the military person involved passing the secrets and his contact. We have to get them. He's ready to give us video on it plus the names. From the info I've gathered, I'm sure no one connected with the brothel is involved with the exception of the Chinese girl, Tao," stated Kemp to the D.A. "In addition he says he has a confession on video of the murder of Norma Santiago at the bank that was robbed here. He says it's all tied to our case."

She thought for a few minutes, asking relevant questions of involvement and knowledge.

"Tell them I'll go along with the immunity for the three of them. June already has it, so it's just those two. But since he's been sitting on this information for who knows how long, I'm not giving witness protection or relocation. I'll contact the state District Attorney who will handle the state charges and let them know the situation and my decision. The three of them will still have to face the residents up there. If they want to move, that's up to them. Let me know if they take it, I'll have to have it emailed to you."

Kemp went back in to give the judge the news.

"Alright, here's the deal the D.A. has authorized. There's no negotiating, this is the last and best; take it or leave it. You will entirely cooperate. No lies, no half-truths. I want complete cooperation. You must also supply all of the information to us you alluded to. If I find out you have lied or held anything back, the deal is off and you will be prosecuted along with your friends."

"And what do I get?"

"She says she will grant total immunity for you, the chief and June from federal and state prosecution, but no relocation or witness protection. If you want to move after this is all over, you move yourself."

"Just like that?" asked Bill.

"Just like that. You got about five minutes to make up your mind or we start heading for Denver."

"Can I talk with the chief or June?"

"No, you will have not have any communication with anyone until we are finished with you…and your stories had better match."

The judge thought for a few minutes. This was the highest stakes poker game he had ever played; should he raise or fold? There was no in between.

"Get me the phone book over there in the cabinet," he said pointing.

"Who are you calling?" asked Kemp.

"My lawyer, I want him to review the agreement before I sign it."

"I'll allow that."

The agent found the phone book and gave it to him. Bill called his lawyer at his home in the Springs and detailed the situation to him.

"Can we meet him in his office in an hour?" asked the Judge.

"Yes, I'll have the agreement emailed to him. What's his email address?" asked Kemp.

The lawyer gave his email address and said he would be waiting at his office.

Kemp called the D.A.'s office and gave the email address to send the immunity agreement to. He also called the agents at the chief's house and told them to stand by and wait for his instructions.

"You three stay here and search the rest of his house," Kemp stated to the agents present.

Kemp and the other two of the agents helped the judge into their black Ford Crown Victoria and put his fold-up wheelchair in the trunk. In an hour they were at his lawyer's office, James R. Peyton, Esquire, in downtown Colorado Springs.

***

Mr. Peyton met them at the door and let them in the street-level office. Introductions were exchanged between Peyton and the three agents.

"The agreement came in about twenty minutes ago. I've been reviewing it and everything seems to be in order as to the details you gave me," Peyton stated to the judge as he handed him a copy.

Bill took a few minutes to review it before signing.

"James, get me the package I mailed to you awhile back. The one I asked you to keep sealed for me in a safe place."

Peyton went to his safe in a rear office and came out with a large manila envelope, still sealed with scotch packaging tape and bearing the tags from the post office of registered mail. He handed it to the judge. "You mean this?"

"Exactly. Here's what you're looking for, Agent Kemp. It starts at one hour and twenty-four minutes."

"Mr. Peyton, do you have a DVD player we could use for a few minutes?" asked Kemp.

"Sure, back here in my office," he said pointing the way.

After being taken to the player, Kemp made a request. "Would you mind if we view this privately with the judge?"

Peyton looked over at the judge who nodded his approval. "I'll be in the waiting room, let me know when your finished," Payton said.

Kemp keyed up the video at one hour and twenty-two minutes.

"Turn up the volume," said the judge, "it may be a bit hard to hear."

They all watched the video intently, no one said a word.

"Is it everything I told you it would be?" asked Tillis.

"It seems to be," stated Kemp.

When they were finished, Kemp called the agents at Bill's house and told them they could call off the search for now and go on back to Denver. He then called his agents at the chief's house and told them to hold up on the search. The three agents there for the search were relieved and told to return to Denver, but the other two were ordered to stay with the chief for now. They could un-cuff him as he now had immunity, courtesy of the judge, but to stay with him until further notice.

***

At the same time Agent Kemp was serving the warrants on the judge, agents were serving warrants on the chief. Reggie was finishing supper by himself when he heard a knock at the door. He opened the door to five men dressed in suits standing on his front porch. He had a queasy feeling in his gut.

"What do you want?" asked the chief boldly. "I take it you're not selling Amway."

"Reginald Campbell?"

"Yeah."

"FBI. We have a warrant for your arrest." Before he could say a word, three of the agents had stepped inside and cuffed him. They patted him down for a weapon and found none.

"Do you have any weapons in the house?" asked an agent.

"Of course I do. I'm the Police Chief, not Barney Fife. What's this all about?"

"You will be informed of the charges when we get you to Denver. For now we have a warrant for your arrest and a search warrant for your house and vehicle. Where are your weapons?"

"Let me see the warrants. Hold them up so I can read them. My gun is over there on the bureau."

"Espionage? Conspiracy? What the fuck are you guys talking about?"

"Just calm down Mr. Campbell, everything will be explained when we get to Denver."

"Get to Denver? What the hell is going on?"

Just then one of the agents received a phone call. When he hung up, he stated, "Have a seat, Mr. Campbell, we're not going to Denver just yet. It seems you may have an angel watching over you."

"What?" The chief was between furious and inquisitive. "I wish you guys would get your shit together and figure out what your doing." This was the chief's worst nightmare, Feds in his house. He hoped they wouldn't find his cash. That would be the end of the world.

Later, the agents received another call from Agent Kemp.

Reggie was un-cuffed and the agents searching the house were sent back to Denver.

"We were told to stay with you until further notice. A couple of our guys are talking with Mr. Tillis. We'll see what happens."

***

Kemp, the two agents and Bill headed back to Cripple Creek with the DVD. On the way Kemp notified the agents staking out the nightclub to be on the lookout for Tao. She would be the next person they would be looking for. He called the office and told them to cancel June's move to Denver, and to cancel the guard on her. There would be no need for either. She could also accept calls and make them.

Kemp also placed a call to Agent Spencer White and told him they had a confession on video of the bank robbery and execution.

"I knew something was screwy about that robbery. There had to be more to it. So it's all tied to your espionage case?"

"Seems to be. I have it all on video. It's a slam dunk."

He gave Kemp the details he had on the vehicles that were in the picture taken in the lot the night before. The front vehicle, the Mazda 626, had to have been Tao's.

Kemp called the agents staking out the nightclub again and gave the details of the two vehicles to be on the lookout for.

Upon arrival at the judge's house, they played the video again. Kemp told the two agents present to relieve the agents at the nightclub and have them come to the judge's house so they could also view the DVD. He wanted them to see what Tao looked like in case she showed up at 'The Club'. They could also see the Colonel and what he looked like, but they needed a name to go along with it. The judge told them a list of names of the customers would be in June's office in the brothel. He gave them the keys to June's office and her elevator card from her purse.

After the other agents had arrived and viewed the DVD, they went back to their surveillance and the other agents returned. "We are leaving for awhile to take care of some business. I want you to stay here and not call anyone until I contact you again, Understand?"

The judge nodded his understanding.

"You've done well for yourself and the others up to this point. Don't screw it up now."

They headed over to the chief's house.

***

When the agents arrived at the chief's house, he was still sitting on his couch waiting for some kind of word as to what was going on.

"Mr. Campbell, I'm Special Agent Kemp. I'm sure you would like to know what is going on."

"I sure as hell would," he snapped back.

"You, June and Mr. Tillis were arrested in association with espionage that was going on in your brothel."

"My brothel, what are you talking about?" asked Reggie, trying to play dumb.

"Mr. Campbell, we know everything about the brothel and nightclub. Both June and Mr. Tillis have given full statements. You are the only one in the dark and you can thank Mr. Tillis for your hind end. He negotiated full immunity for all three of you with the United States District Attorney and the local District Attorney. Now all you have to do is completely cooperate and we'll soon be done here."

"Let me call the judge for a minute."

"Go ahead."

The chief made his phone call.

"Bill, what the hell is going on?"

"Reggie, it all has to do with something you didn't know about. I'm sorry it got all of us involved, but there isn't anything any of us could have done. I'm glad at this point we have the DVD's, it saved all of our asses."

"What DVD's? What are you talking about?"

"June knows about them. We kept it from you and Dan. We had cameras put in all the rooms in the brothel years ago. June brought me the DVD's every Thursday. I have a library of them."

"Son-of-a-bitch, after all I've done, you keep this from me?" he yelled.

"I know I should have told you, but...it saved our asses, Reggie. There a guy we know as the Colonel. He's been passing NORAD information to Tao, our China Girl, who passed it on to the Chinese. We have to get his real name out of June's office and I think they will be done with us. Cooperate with them fully and we'll be out of this mess. Don't lie to them and screw up our immunity deal."

"I'll take them down there. The sooner they're out of my house, the better."

CHAPTER 40

The chief escorted Agent Kemp and the other two agents to the nightclub. Although the nightclub was open for business, the brothel would not be open for another couple of hours. Kemp told the two agents surveilling 'The Club' to keep watch while they went in. Reggie swiped his card in the elevator and rode it down to the brothel.

"Nice place," Kemp stated. "Pretty fancy."

"It was," returned the chief.

They went directly to June's office. The chief opened the filing cabinet containing all the customer's files and their backgrounds, which he had personally investigated. He found the file they were looking for. **Colonel John Durham, U.S. Air Force, Space Command, NORAD, Cheyenne Mountain, Colorado Springs**.

"This was too easy," said Agent Kemp, "After all these months, everything we needed was right here." He grabbed the folder and looked at the contents; a picture, a police NCIC report, some hand-written notes detailing his sexual preferences and the girls he preferred, most notably Tao.

Kemp was on his cell phone within seconds to the D.A. He found he had no signal, probably because they were in the lower level.

"Give me everything you have on Tao, also," Kemp demanded.

Reggie went through another drawer and found Tao's file.

"This is everything we have on her," he stated, "The address and phone number is about a year old and may not be up-to-date."

Kemp looked at the file. There wasn't much besides a picture and some basic background information.

"Let's get out of here," he said, "I want this place closed up tighter than a virgin's ass."

They rode the elevator back to the main floor and went outside. Immediately, Kemp was on his cell phone again to the D.A.

"His name is Colonel John Durham, assigned to NORAD. I'm sending agents down to pick him up right now." He listened for a moment then said, "No, we don't have a positive address on her as yet. I have an address and phone number, but he doesn't know if it is up to date. Might be though. All right, I'll let you know what happens."

Kemp instructed the two agents watching the place to call the Sheriff's Department for assistance, shut the whole place down, including the nightclub, and seal it. It now belonged to the Federal government.

"What do you mean, it belongs to the Feds?" asked the chief.

"It was involved in foreign espionage, it now belongs to the U.S. Government."

"But you gave us immunity."

"That's right, but there was no agreement about you keeping the nightclub and brothel. Look, you can take it to court and explain to a judge or a jury what you had going on here, explain our agreement, and see if you can win that argument, but I wouldn't if I were you."

Reggie knew that it certainly would be a lost cause. He thought about how it would look before a judge, *"Well, you see, your Honor, we wee running an underground whorehouse with our nightclub. We had a Chinese spy on our payroll and the government came in and took it all away. We'd like to have it all back".* No, he knew that dog just wouldn't hunt. He dropped it.

***

The nightclub was closed down and all the feds had left for the Springs. The chief called Bill. They had a lot to discuss and decided to do it over a few drinks. Reggie drove to the judge's house to pick him up. They would go to Ralf's. No one in the city knew yet they had been arrested, released, and given immunity, but this would probably be the last trip anywhere in the city where they could show their faces. When Reggie got to Bill's house, they took his van back into the city to Ralf's.

As Reggie drove, to break the silence he asked the judge, "Did you know that June's son, Thomas, was actually Dan's kid?"

The judge laughed. "Where'd you hear that?"

"I found Dan's Will in his desk. He left everything to his son, Thomas."

The judge laughed harder. "That's just what Dan thought. He never had a paternity test done. June let him think Thomas was his son because she needed the child support at the time. She couldn't make it on a librarian's salary. She never had the heart to tell him that he really wasn't his kid."

"Son-of-a-bitch," yelled Reggie.

"June and Dan had an affair a long time ago. When it came out, it led to Dan's divorce. When she got pregnant, Dan just naturally assumed the kid was his."

"I never knew he was married. So, whose kid is it?"

"I don't really know. She was seeing a couple guys at the time, maybe having a couple affairs. It'll probably remain one of those eternal mysteries."

"Well, I know who the kid looks like," smiled the chief looking at the judge.

"I don't want to know," Bill replied.

CHAPTER 41

They arrived at Ralf's and parked in the handicap zone directly in front of the restaurant. The chief helped the judge with his wheelchair into the bar.

Roxie and Ted were both tending bar. It was to be Ted's last night and he was going to tell Roxie he was an undercover FBI agent. He would tell her at the end of the shift. He was dreading it as he had been lying to her all this time and he kind of liked her.

"What'll it be, gents?" Roxie yelled across the bar.

"The regular, Roxie," the chief replied.

Ted brought the drinks over to the table; the judge his Jack and Coke, and the chief a bottle of Bud.

Raising his bottle the chief said, "Here's to my last day as Police Chief. Tomorrow I resign." They both toasted.

"And here's to my last day as a judge!" They both toasted again.

"Who do you think ratted us out? How do you think they found out about us?" ask Tillis.

"Hell, I don't know, but I'd bet it was that asshole Dan. He was drinking again and getting paranoid. Who else could it be?"

"I think they got to June, but I can't blame her. She had to protect her kids. I kinda felt sorry for her being put in a position to have to choose between us and her kids."

"Okay, now that our club is done, you have to tell me, who are the other three partners of 'The Club' you'd never tell us about? Did they also get immunity?" asked Reggie.

"Nope."

"Why didn't you cover them?"

Bill laughed. "You really want to know?" he asked, "You're not going to like what I'm going to tell you and you're really going to be pissed off at me."

"I am? Why?"

The judge laughed and took a long drink. He mentally debated whether he should tell him.

"Cause there aren't any other partners," he finally stated.

"What? What about the telephone conversations, the jury sessions?" he asked.

"I hired a schmuck in the Springs to play the part and told him what to say."

Reggie was silent for several moments. "Why'd you do it?" he asked.

The judge laughed again. "Hell, I got the cut for three other people that didn't exist! But I also put a lot more money in it than you, June, and Dan. I just thought it would be easier that way than to argue for a bigger cut."

"Then it was you that gave Dan the death penalty?"

"Yeah, it was me. I'm not proud of it, but I really felt he was going to rat us out and I guess I was right."

The chief thought about it for a minute and decided to let it all go. At this point it was water under the bridge. Besides, he had Dan's cut, the two hundred thousand dollars, and Bill didn't know anything about it! The joke was on him and he didn't even know it! That alone would make up for the three extra cuts the judge got. Now he didn't feel bad about not splitting the cash he stole from Dan's house with Bill. He realized they were all fucking each other.

"If I had found out about it earlier, I'd have been really pissed, but now..."

The chief stopped in mid-sentence. A man he recognized as one of the Red Lantern's customers had just walked through the front door.

"Bill, look who just walked in."

***

The Colonel had come up for another drop to China Doll, but saw the nightclub was closed again. He had noticed two Asian men dressed in suits hanging around the nightclub, and felt uneasy about it. He decided to stroll around for a while; hoping China Doll would find him again, just like the last time.

"Hey, isn't that the Colonel?" Reggie whispered to judge.

"It sure as hell is," he responded. "You're still the Chief of Police, maybe you should go arrest him."

"No way in hell I'm getting involved in any more of this. Far as I'm concerned, we never saw him. You can call Kemp if you want; I've got his card here."

The judge thought a minute. "Fuck 'em."

***

The Colonel sat down at a table in the front restaurant area of Ralf's and picked up a menu. He saw the two Asian-looking men he had seen near the nightclub come through the front door and take seats to the rear of him. He dismissed them as tourists, just two of many Asians who visited the city.

One of the men got up and walked towards the restroom, but stopped at the bar. He stood looking back at the other Asian man who then got up from his seat, and marched up behind the Colonel. He pulled out a black revolver with a silencer attached, and put it to the back of the Colonel's head.

Thump. Thump. Thump. Three muffled shots broke the relative tranquility of the soft background music.

The Colonel slumped over onto the table, blood gushing from the back of his head. The gunman started to place the revolver on the table when the chief stood up and pulled his pearl-handled, chrome-plated, 9mm Smith and Wesson from under his jacket.

"Police, drop it," he yelled, pointing the automatic towards the gunman. The chief had tunnel vision induced by the stress of the moment and he completely forgot about the second Asian man by the bar. The gunman, who had murdered the Colonel, quickly turned toward Reggie and fired two shots. Thump, thump. He missed. The Chief returned fire with three rounds. The blasts from the high velocity, un-silenced rounds rang in everyone's ears, two of the rounds hitting the gunman in the abdomen and chest. The third round hit the large picture window in front of Ralf's, shattering the window. Large glass fragments crashed to the concrete sidewalk outside and smashed onto tables and chairs inside.

By now, everyone in Ralf's was on the floor except for the judge. He couldn't move; he was strapped in his chair. All he could do was watch.

The Asian man by the bar, was only about ten feet away. He pulled a revolver that was also was silenced-and fired two rounds at the Chief. Thump. Thump. He hit the Chief twice, once in the head and once in the chest. The blood spurted out from the Chief's forehead like a small fountain as he slowly slumped to the floor. Bill tried to reach for the chief's gun that had fallen on the floor next to him, but couldn't reach it. Thump.

***

Ted had been stocking beer in the cooler in back of the bar when the shooting erupted. He hadn't heard the silenced shots, but he knew what he heard when the chief fired off three rounds. As he came out of the cooler, he saw the chief on the ground and a man heading quickly towards the door. He saw the revolver in his right hand, and pulled his Smith and Wesson Chief's Special .38 from inside his boot.

"FBI. Freeze!" he yelled. The man turned toward Ted and started to raise his silenced revolver. Ted fired three shots in an instant, dropping the Asian like a dead fish. It was over.

The customers who had been eating supper in the front restaurant area of Ralf's ran out the front door, some screaming. Roxie ran over to Reggie, and checked for his pulse. He was dead.

Roxie then looked at the judge who was still sitting in his wheelchair. His eyes were open, staring towards the front door, but he wasn't moving. His arms were down by his sides.

"Judge? Judge, you okay?"

She shook him a little and noticed a bright red spot in the center of his chest.

"Ted, I think the judge is dead too."

Ted checked for a pulse. There was none.

"He's gone. He was probably hit in the crossfire from the initial exchange of gunfire between the Chief and the first gunman."

Roxie then turned towards Ted. "FBI?" she asked, mouth agape. "What the fuck? You asshole!"

"I was going to tell you tonight. Let's talk about it later."

"You're a son-of-a-bitch."

"I know, but, please, not now. You can call me all the names you want later. Let's help who we can now."

Weapon still at the ready, Ted carefully walked over to the two Chinese men and kicked away their revolvers. The Colonel's assassin was still alive, but barely. He was losing blood fast.

"Roxie, call the station and get the police and an ambulance down here."

"You giving orders now?" she asked sarcastically.

"Roxie, please."

"Okay, okay!"

Roxie called the police station emergency number she had on speed dial she always called when there was a bar fight. She never called 911; that always took her to the Sheriff's department. It always took longer to get the cops as the Sheriff's department then had to call the local police.

Ted applied pressure on the assassin's wound hoping to stop the bleeding. He wanted him alive and able to be questioned.

"Cripple Creek Police, can I help you?"

"This is Roxie at Ralf's Breakroom. Please send some officers and the ambulance, we've had a shooting and I think four people are dead."

"Who is this?"

"*Roxie* at Ralf's Breakroom," she yelled. "Please hurry!"

"You better not be playing with me, Roxie. What you're saying is serious."

"*NO SHIT!!* Send the damn police. *NOW!*"

"I'll notify the sergeant, but you better not be lying to me."

***

Sgt. Majors and Officer Sanborn were filling their patrol car with gas at the Public Works barn on the southwest side of town when the call came.

"Headquarters to Sgt. Majors."

"Majors, go ahead."

"I have a report of shots fired at Ralf's Breakroom. She states she believes four people are dead. You better get down there."

"Who reported it?"

"She says her name is Roxie."

"Roxie called? 10-4. You better get an ambulance started. Call the Sheriff's Department and let them know also."

"Will do."

"Holy shit, Frank, think it's real?" asked Chris.

"Probably is. I've known Roxie for a long time; she wouldn't bullshit about something like this."

Frank stopped filling the vehicle and they headed for Ralf's immediately.

The ambulance and Majors arrived at the bar simultaneously. Majors didn't know what to expect as he entered, but observed bodies all over the place. The bartender, Ted, had a .38 revolver in his hand.

"Drop it!" yelled Majors. "Drop it now!"

Ted looked up to see two officers pointing their weapons at him.

Ted bent down and placed the revolver on the floor while telling them, "Don't shoot, I'm an FBI agent!" He kept his hands in the air.

"Yeah, and I'm the Pope," said Majors.

Roxie immediately came over and stepped in front of Ted. "Frank, he IS an FBI agent! Put your guns away!"

"You have some identification?" asked Majors.

"In my boot."

"Slow and easy does it," he said.

Ted retrieved his identification and tossed it to Frank. "So it's Steve, not Ted."

"Yeah, can you lower those weapons? I don't want any accidents happening; especially to me."

Throwing the ID back to Steve, he motioned to Chris, "He's good." They holstered their weapons and Ted picked his back up.

"What the hell is going on here?" He took a few more steps into the restaurant where he suddenly saw the wheelchair with a body in it.

"Is that the judge?" he asked.

"Yeah, it looks like he took a stray one from the Chinese agent when he was shooting at the chief," Steve replied.

"Chinese agent? What the hell are you talking about?"

Steve chuckled, "I'll tell you all about it. First, let's get organized. We still have one alive."

"And the chief?" he asked standing over the body.

"One of the Chinese agents got him after the chief shot the other one. It all seemed to happen at once. It's a long story, so you better get some help down here. It's going to be a long night."

Majors called headquarters on his cell phone. "Tell the Sheriff's department to put a move on it. Tell them to send a few extra men if they can spare it. Call the CBI and tell them to get down here and call the Medical Examiner's office."

"You really have four dead bodies?" asked dispatch

"Probably three. Just do what I ask. And keep all this off the radio. Call me on my cell phone if you need me."

"Will do and right away. Should I call the chief, too? He's going to want to be notified."

Majors searched for a way to say no, but not tell the dispatcher he was dead. "No need; he's already here."

The ambulance crew prepared the gunman who was still alive for a life flight and started removing him.

"Hold on a minute, guys," Steve yelled from across the room. "I have to search him before you haul his ass out of here."

Steve did a thorough search of the assassin, coming up only with his wallet containing a driver's license, some car keys and a photo of the Major. His name was Won Hung Lo. The license was from California.

Big surprise there, thought Steve.

***

Chris then taped off the area around Ralf's with yellow police tape. No one except law enforcement was allowed in.

Sgt. Majors, being the next ranking officer of the police department, assumed command of the department and the grizzly scene.

***

"I have to call this in," said Steve.

Steve called Special Agent Kemp who was in the Springs trying to find the Colonel.

"Agent Kemp, you better get up here. We've got a mess."

"My men are about to raid the Colonel's house, can't it wait?"

"You don't need to be in a big hurry, the raid can wait; I've got him here."

"You've got him in custody?"

"Sort of."

"What?"

"He's dead."

"He's dead?"

"Yeah, he took three to the head from what I believe is a Chinese agent. There were two of them. They must have been trying to clean up some loose ends. I've got one dead and another who I shot, but he's still hanging on. The paramedics are prepping him now for a trip to Memorial Hospital in the Springs via Life Flight."

"Okay, you handle the situation up there for now. I'll send you more men and the shooting team. I'm going to the hospital. We have to protect what's left. I'm sure they may try to neutralize him."

"Will do," Steve acknowledged.

"Be sure to check the Colonel's body for any documents, disks, thumb-drives or anything suspicious before they remove it. I don't know how he was transferring the data; it could be on anything or in anything. If he was in Cripple Creek, it had to be to deliver more stolen classified info from NORAD. We don't want that info falling into anyone else's hands, Also, look for a black Pontiac Grand Am, probably registered out-of-state. If you find it, impounded at once and sealed it. We'll search it later."

"Got it. I need to find the Chinese assassin's vehicle, too. What's the status on Tao, have you found her place yet?"

"We went to her last known address a couple hours ago. Turns out she still lived there but we were too late. She was assassinated also, probably about an hour before we got there. We weren't able to find her vehicle or driver's license in the Colorado registry because both were from California. I've got a team going through her place and her car as we speak."

CHAPTER 42

Adam was at home and when he heard all the sirens. He turned on his police scanner but didn't hear a thing, which he thought was unusual. He decided to walk downtown with his notepad and camera and snoop around. When he arrived on Bennett Ave, he saw a multitude of red and blue lights from the various police vehicles and ambulances at the other end of town. Adam headed there at a brisk walk. He arrived at Ralf's to a taped off area around the building.

Adam wasn't allowed inside the taped area, but Steve observed him and came outside to see him.

"What the hell is going on, Steve?"

"All hell broke loose, Adam. Both the chief and the judge are dead along with what I believe is a Chinese agent. The person who was passing the sensitive military data is also dead. One of the Chinese agents is shot, but still alive. I have to go for now, but I'll brief you later."

"Thanks."

Adam called Brian who immediately came down to the bar. Adam briefed him on what he knew.

"What have I done?" Brian asked pacing back and forth.

"What do you mean?" asked Adam.

"This is all because of me. If I hadn't started asking questions, this never would have happened."

"Brian, this happened because they were all corrupt. It has nothing to do with you. If they hadn't been operating a brothel in town, none of this would have occurred."

"I suppose your right, Adam, but I still feel bad about it." The pastor said some silent prayers for the departed.

"It's kind of funny, you know. The chief played the good guy in the end, protecting the public--and the judge, he was just an innocent victim."

"Probably the only times in their lives they were innocent or victims," Adam replied. "In the wrong place at the wrong time. Karma."

***

Steve searched the Colonel's body but didn't find any documents or items that could contain stolen data.

"Sgt. Majors, would you direct your men and the Sheriff's department to look for a black Pontiac Grand Am in the area. If it is found, please notify me immediately. The vehicle is not to be touched. I have to seal it and have it towed to our garage for processing. Also, I have some keys to a newer Ford from one of the assassins. If you can spare someone soon, we need to go around the area and see if the remote will trigger a car alarm. If it does, I'll need to impound that vehicle too."

The Grand Am was discovered down the street within a few minutes. Steve called it in and had it impounded and towed. It, too, had California plates. An hour later a Ford F-150 with California plates responded to the remote. It was impounded and towed also.

Several hours later the FBI, CBI, and Sheriff's Department were still photographing the crime scene and interviewing witnesses. Steve thought this would be a good time to talk to Roxie who was still shaken up from the shootout. He found her sitting outside on the curb.

"I was going to talk to you tonight. This was going to be my last night here. Our investigation was finished so I was free to explain everything to you," Steve told her.

"Well, in a way I'm really pissed off at you, but, I'm glad you were here. I don't know what to be right now. Is Ted even your real name?"

"My real name is Steve, Steven Coats."

"Steven Coats. Son-of-a-bitch."

"Now," Steve said, "I've got one question for you before I have to leave. Who's been notching the beam above the bar and what are they for?"

"That's two questions." Roxie blushed. Steve knew he had her.

"Okay, Mr. FBI, you got me. Take me away." She was smiling. She put her arms out, but didn't say any more.

"Well, what are they?"

"You're such a great investigator, you tell me," she said teasing him.

"Okay, I think they're your tally, of, how should I say it, of conquests?"

She laughed. "You're close."

"Come on, tell me. I haven't got time for a hundred questions."

"Okay, okay." She hesitated, smiling and looking directly at Steve. "They're my *younger* conquests." Then she said in a hushed voice with just a little bit of a smirk, "You didn't count."

This time it was Steve's turn to blush.

"All in the line of duty," he said saluting Roxie, "All in the line of duty."

"Yeah, right."

"But, really, that's between us."

***

Gradually, the town filled with reporters and television cameras trying to get the big story. Three hours later, every television station from Colorado Springs and Denver were present along with other national news organizations. Word had definitely leaked out. All they could *officially* ascertain was there was a shootout at Ralf's, where the window was shot out, and there were three dead individuals. No identifications were formally given, but word had leaked out that the Police Chief and the judge were among the casualties.

Later news releases from the State Police stated a shooting of a high-ranking military officer had taken place at Ralf's and the police chief and judge had been killed trying to stop the shooters.

CHAPTER 43

Dark clouds were gathering in the distance to the west, although it was clear and sunny at the moment and the temperature hovered around forty-five degrees in the shade. Adam was concerned about the possibility of the clouds opening up while he and Jenny were out on their first spring horseback ride. Spring storms tended to come in fast and hard in the mountains. He and his daughter would have no cover against the cold rain and wind that would accompany such weather.

Their horses were fat and lazy from being fed sweet grain and alfalfa hay throughout the winter months. They needed the exercise.

Adam's six-year-old daughter, Jenny, was going riding with him today. She had been riding horses since she was old enough to hold on.

"Daddy, I've wanted to be a cowgirl my whooole life!" she exclaimed to Adam, as she rushed to get ready to go riding with him. "When will I be a real cowgirl?"

Adam laughed as he pulled on his boots and headed outside to round up the horses.

"You already are, honey. Just look at you, you're the prettiest looking cowgirl I've ever seen!"

Today Jenny had dressed herself in her most "cowgirly" attire. She was wearing a white hat and matching white boots. Her golden brown hair was braided into two pigtails, the ends resting at the front of her shoulders. She wore black wrangler jeans and dressed in a western detailed shirt.

It was obvious to Adam that Jenny was excited about going riding with him. She dragged out all of Sir

Danton's tack she could carry. Grabbing a currycomb she quickly set to grooming him.

Sir Danton was Jenny's horse, a twelve-year-old bay Davenport Arabian. Adam had purchased him for a hundred and fifty dollars after his daughter fell instantly in love with him. That was three years ago.

Davenport Arabians are smaller than other Arabian breeds and this one had turned out to be the perfect horse for Jenny. He was bombproof. Nothing spooked him. He had obviously been well trained by a previous owner.

It had been a love affair between the two of them ever since, and Jenny was always riding him around the small ranch they owned. Sir Danton showed Jenny the affection that only a child could appreciate. Whenever she went outside, he would see her, and would instantly start walking towards her. He followed her everywhere he could. Jenny would go to him and he would nuzzle and rub her face with his, which she loved, and would reward him with apple-flavored treats.

Adam's mount was Bo, a five-year-old light brown and white Palomino paint. Adam had been present at Bo's birth and had helped to break him as a two year old, purchasing him shortly thereafter. Bo had become a great trail horse. There were still some undesirable traits to overcome with him, as he would spook once in a while at unfamiliar noises or objects. Bo really didn't like fire hydrants; they were monsters to be avoided.

**

The deep ravines of the mountains north of Cripple Creek were some of Adam's favorite places to ride. The sun was just high enough in the sky to reach the depths of the narrow valleys. The small streams of icy, clear water flowed on the lowest parts of the mountain floor, gurgling as they journeyed over the rocky streambeds.

A mountain breeze, cooled by the remaining snow and channeled though the ravine, chilled their exposed skin.

The trees hadn't started to bud yet. At about ten thousand feet the aspen wouldn't start budding until the middle of May. The horses were sure-footed, but slipped once in a while on the patches of slick wet snow that remained from the spring storms.

Today was the first time Jenny rode with her father in his favorite ravine, and he was watching her intently. "Jenny, remember to keep your heels down, and put your hands closer to the horn," Adam gently reminded her.

"Like this, daddy?" asked Jenny.

"Great, Jenny, You've got it."

The ravine they were exploring was deep, approximately six hundred feet below Highway 67. The highway above was formerly a railroad bed. It had been cutout from the side of the mountain, shelf like. In the late 1890's, trains were used to pick up gold ore from the mines in Cripple Creek and Victor. The ore would then be transported to the stamping mills in Colorado Springs, where the gold was processed into gold bullion. The last remaining railroad tunnel to Cripple Creek had been closed to traffic in 1995, when the walls started to cave in. The tunnel was condemned and a new two-lane road was built around it.

The pine and aspen trees were thick on the hillsides. Boulders sat perched precariously all the way up past the road; some appeared as though a small breeze would loosen and send them rolling down to the bottom of the ravine. Every once in a while, a rockslide would close the highway. A road crew would use heavy machinery to push the rocks over the edge of the road and send them bouncing down the hillside, destroying everything in their path, many to end up in the ravine they were riding in.

As Adam and Jenny continued their ride, the horses hesitated, their heads high and ears pricked up. They were looking up the hill. Their eyes were wide open with the whites showing, nostrils flared. As they nudged the horses to go forward, Bo and Sir Danton started prancing, turning their bodies toward the hill, snorting. Adam knew something was wrong. He had experienced this before when there was a bear in the area. The horses could smell a bear or a mountain lion long before humans would see it.

"Daddy, why won't Sir Danton go?"

"He senses or smells something, Jenny, let's just wait here a minute."

"Daddy, look," Jenny said, "There's something big up there on the hill."

Adam looked in the direction Jenny was pointing and saw a large object about two hundred feet in front of them, partially covered in snow. Whatever it was, it was lodged between a large granite boulder on one side and several aspen trees on the other.

"Jenny, wait here with the horses. I'm going to go check it out." He dismounted Bo and tied the reins to a small aspen tree.

As Adam walked closer, he could tell it was an older white Chevy Blazer turned on its side, the rear of the SUV facing him. As he closed the remaining distance to the car at a quicker pace, he studied the vehicle. It looked familiar to him, but he couldn't quite place it. He climbed the hillside to the car, his boots trying to get a foothold, slipping and sliding in the remaining snow and loose gravel.

There were claw marks on the door and top of the vehicle; several different types. Adam knew there were bears, coyotes and mountain lions in the area, but why would they be clawing at a car? There could only be one reason. It immediately struck him as he inhaled the putrid stench of decaying flesh. He suddenly remembered who had a Blazer like the one he was looking at.

CHAPTER 44

Adam climbed up and around the vehicle, holding on to the numerous tree saplings that filled the hillside, to the top of the Chevy. He looked at the damaged front end and observed animal hair protruding from areas of the front grille. *Elk*, he thought to himself, *or maybe deer*.

Travelers along highway 67 were always hitting elk, sometimes killing the driver as their huge body came over the hood of the car and slammed through the windshield.

Adam brushed the heavy wet snow away from the cracked windshield and looked inside. He wasn't prepared for the grotesque, twisted image in the car. The look of horror staring back at him from inside the vehicle was something Adam would never forget. It would be forever frozen in his memory, as it was frozen throughout the winter on the face of the corpse inside. It was Dan, the ex-mayor.

Adam turned and hurried down the hill to his horse. He felt the blood had drained from his face and his mind was racing with questions. What was the fastest way back? Where could he get a cell signal? Who should he report it to, and what should he tell Jenny?

Adam decided to call the Sheriff's Department once he could get a signal on his cell as it was in the county and if there was any hanky-panky involved, he wanted the Sheriff's Department to be the investigating entity.

"What's wrong, daddy?" Jenny could tell her father was acting different.

"That's a car you found, Jenny, and it belongs to someone who's been missing for several months. We have to go tell someone what you found." Adam didn't want Jenny to know about the Mayor's body inside. She would have nightmares for months.

"Do we have to go now? Can't we ride some more?" she whined.

"We'll go again tomorrow, Jenny, but we have to go back now."

Adam knew Jenny didn't understand. He saw tears welling up in her eyes and tried to console her.

"But daddy," she protested, "I've been waiting all week to go riding with you. Stupid car, it's not fair," Jenny pouted.

"I know, honey, but sometimes things happen we can't control. We have to tell somebody about the car you found. You're going to be a hero. Some people might even ask how you discovered it, and you can tell them how you were just being a cowgirl, out riding Sir Danton when you found it. How cool is that?"

Jenny perked up, she smiled, and her eyes brightened. Now everyone would know she was a real cowgirl!

EPILOGUE

The FBI never did release all of the details to the press pertaining to the espionage, which ended with the deaths of six people.

The wounded Chinese agent that assassinated the Colonel died of his wounds two days later. They were never able to interrogate him.

The chief had died a hero, along with the judge, defending the citizens of Cripple Creek. Adam decided to leave it that way.

The ex-Mayor had definitely died in an accident. He had hit an elk on a snowy road sending him down a three hundred foot embankment. Hair from the elk was still lodged in the grill of his car. A dead bull elk was found several hundred feet from the buried vehicle.

Adam was the only one who had the whole story and was torn over whether to write it or not; it would have made national headlines and given him a boost in his credentials. In the end, he decided against it, as June's children would be the ones to have paid the largest price.

The pastor never did speak of the incident again, preferring not to remember how the whole story was started. He still blamed himself for a string of events that ended in the death of many people.

June applied for and was appointed executor of the estates of her friends; Dan, the chief and the judge. The chief, also not having any living relatives, had left his entire estate to his three partners, June, the judge and the Mayor, Dan Comeau. Dan, of course, had left his entire estate to the son he thought he had, Thomas Perry, June's son.

The judge also left his entire estate to his son, Thomas Perry. June knew where both had hidden their cash throughout the years and before selling their houses, found over one million dollars between the two, in addition to the thirty thousand left behind at Dan's house by the chief.

And the judge's library? Well, that's another story.

One of the old parlour houses still remains today as it was years ago, only, as a local museum. The Old Homestead House Museum is a tribute to the Madams and ladies of the night of Cripple Creek's Gold Rush days. Its location on Myers Avenue is just south of the main thoroughfare of Bennett Avenue. It was rebuilt with brick after the fire of 1895 that destroyed a good part of the city, and flourished as a brothel until 1917.

Today, the building is tucked neatly between a casino and a parking lot. It is rather non-descript, until you enter it.

The City and museum curators have preserved the house and its furnishings to exhibit to tourists during the summer months. Though the carpets are worn, even threadbare in some places, it is easy to imagine the decadence and charm that existed nightly during its heyday, when ladies of the evening completely entertained the wealthy gentlemen of yesteryear. It's even rumored that the ghosts of the "painted ladies" still haunt the house late at night. The heavy velvet drapes are drawn tight at night, and sounds of those souls long past have been heard emanating from its rooms. The night evokes such memories here; it is said that the present never changes; only the past is repeated.

Timothy M. BRAUN

Author of
WHEN THE ANGELS CRY
The Story of Arielle
An exciting, thought provoking, inspirational novel!
Readers agree, this story will change your life!
Have you ever received a miracle?

If you liked *"The Shack"* by Wm. Paul Young or the *"Joshua"* series by Joseph F. Girzone, then you'll love *WHEN THE ANGELS CRY—The Story of Arielle*.

"WHEN THE ANGELS CRY—The Story of Arielle" is an intriguing novel with a variety of phenomenal turns." Diane Niebling, Nebraska

Recommended reading by the Colonia del Rey Book Club.

Read **When The Angels Cry—The Story of Arielle** and discover the miracles in your life. Go to www.whentheangelscry.com to read sample chapters of this exiting book!

MIRACLE OR COINCIDENCE?
Have you ever been the recipient of a miracle? Most of us probably have, whether we know it or not. Think back.

How many critical situations can you recall affecting yourself or your family in which a crisis was averted? Divine intervention or twist of fate?

THE INFANT

After losing her own child to S.I.D.S. and in a deep depression, Rebecca finds Arielle on her doorstep as an infant, but possessing something so mysterious Rebecca finds it hard to comprehend. She starts to question her own sanity. As Arielle grows, Rebecca observes her daughter in conversations with an invisible presence.

MESSAGES FROM THE ANGELS

While helping a friend, Arielle is injured and placed in extreme danger. She struggles with her own resolve.

Throughout her childhood, she is barraged with questions from religious leaders who have difficulty accepting Rebecca's observations, and Arielle's angelic messages to them. The leaders are told they must change their lives, attitudes, and behaviors; start believing in and teaching about a loving, compassionate God.

After a dispute with a teacher at her school that escalates to litigation, Arielle is faced with a judge who has no tolerance for religious matters.

Who is this child? Will they ever believe her? Will they do what they are asked?

To order a book with free shipping, Go to:
http://mainstreet-colorado.com/when-the-angels-cry-the-story-of-arielle-free-shipping/

Timothy M. Braun, the author of the fast-selling *When The Angels Cry* crosses genres and brings you a thrilling, new non-stop novel that will keep you up at night!

The Contest
You Can't Leave 'Till It's Over

You are invited with nine other writers to a contest sponsored by an agency that represents new authors. It is to be held in Aspen, Colorado with all expenses paid. "The Prize of Your Life", $60,000, and a publishing contract will be awarded to the winner. Would you turn it down?

George Hearthstone relates to a retired homicide detective, Sergeant Rico Sanducci, a chilling story he says he has lived through, but no one will believe him. George is in a private mental institution, and Mack can't figure out if his story is true or a figment of his imagination and drugs. George swears by it, but the police say they can't authenticate any of it.

"To say this was a strange case would be like saying the sun rises in the east. If his story is true, they were like rats in a cage, with the captors constantly poking them with sticks. The decisions they were made to make—the ethical choices alone would make anyone question their own moral compass. Was it some kind of social experiment, a sick joke that got out of hand, or more like I believe, an organization that preys on vulnerable people?"
- Mack Salmon

Book Reviews

Braun's New Book is a Dark Thriller

Cripple Creek writer Timothy Braun has written a gritty second novel, "The Contest."

Photo by Norma Engelberg

Teller County News

Posted: Thursday, November 10, 2011 2:30 pm

By Norma Engelberg | 0 comments

Timothy Braun's latest book, "The Contest," is the direct opposite of his last work of literature.

The previous book, "When Angels Cry: The Story of Arielle," was about an angel come to earth. "The Contest," meanwhile, is a gritty mystery that has a lot more of the Devil in it and keeps its readers guessing even beyond the book's ending.

George Russo is an aspiring writer whose novel has been rejected more times than he would like to admit. He is confident that his book is good and could be a best seller but agents won't even take a look at it. Just when he hits rock bottom — out of money and living in a worse-than-ratty New York City hotel room, he gets an invitation to enter a writing contest with a prize of $60,000.

At the end of his rope, he jumps at the chance despite several misgivings and he is selected as one of the 10 contestants. Thus begins Russo's trials as he endures two months in a ghost town in the middle of unidentified nowhere with limited power, water and food and a murderer who leaves vicious poetry on the graves that he leaves in his wake.

The book is slow starting but once all the contestants come together, it catches the imagination and turns into a page-turner. The contestants, however — seven men and three women — are as flawed as the contest they've entered. Russo, Stewart and Paul are the most likeable, Harry is an unmitigated jerk — the other contestants have worse names for him — and Dorothy, despite her issues, turns out to be a pretty good companion.

Readers should be aware that true to its nature, this book's language is as far from angelic as its characters.

Braun brings his law enforcement background into play in this tense mystery. Who are the contest's patrons, why are they so cruel and what do they want? Russo wants to know and by the end so will readers.

Braun, the real-life author, splits his time between Cripple Creek and Corpus Christi, Texas. He has been a crypto-analyst for the Army Security Agency, a detective sergeant in a Massachusetts police department, owned and wrote for the Gold Camp Journal in Cripple Creek and served on the Cripple Creek-Victor RE-1 School Board. He is currently working on a sequel to his first book, "When Angels Cry: In the Line of Fire."

To order a book with free shipping, Go to:

http://mainstreet-colorado.com/the-contest-you-cant-leave-till-its-over-free-shipping/

WATCH FOR:

WHEN THE ANGELS CRY
In The Line of Fire

(The Second in a Series)

As a small boy growing up, Jacob tells adults about conversations he has with angels, but no one believes him. He enters school and encounters a special teacher.

As an adult, he becomes a police officer. With his supernatural ties, he tackles situations in a world of corruption, drugs, death and mayhem that no one would want to encounter. An angel with human emotions, he must circumvent the natural desires of humanity and make decisions that would test the mettle of anyone, yet maintain his special relationship with the Almighty.